R.I.P.
SCOOT

Sara Flemington

R.I.P. SCOOT

NIGHTWOOD EDITIONS

2025

Copyright © Sara Flemington, 2025

1 2 3 4 5 — 29 28 27 26 25

ALL RIGHTS RESERVED. No part of this publication may be reproduced, stored in a retrieval system or transmitted, in any form or by any means, without prior permission of the publisher or, in the case of photocopying or other reprographic copying, a licence from Access Copyright, the Canadian Copyright Licensing Agency, www.accesscopyright.ca, info@accesscopyright.ca.

Nightwood Editions
P.O. Box 1779
Gibsons, BC V0N 1V0
Canada
www.nightwoodeditions.com

COVER DESIGN: Anna Comfort O'Keeffe
TYPOGRAPHY: Rafael Chimicatti

Nightwood Editions acknowledges the support of the Canada Council for the Arts, the Government of Canada, and the Province of British Columbia through the BC Arts Council.

This book has been printed on 100% post-consumer recycled paper.

Printed and bound in Canada.

LIBRARY AND ARCHIVES CANADA CATALOGUING IN PUBLICATION

Title: R.I.P. Scoot / Sara Flemington.
Other titles: Rest in peace Scoot
Names: Flemington, Sara, author.
Identifiers: Canadiana (print) 20240522346 | Canadiana (ebook) 20240523555 | ISBN 9780889714823 (softcover) | ISBN 9780889714830 (EPUB)
Subjects: LCGFT: Novels.
Classification: LCC PS8611.L435 R57 2025 | DDC C813/.6—dc23

For Cheesy.
We love you. We miss you.
Thanks for writing this book with me.

Contents

CHAPTER 1
The Arrival 9

CHAPTER 2
A New Key 25

CHAPTER 3
Gross Garbage All Over the Ground 41

CHAPTER 4
Chamomile Tea and Half a Million Dollars 61

CHAPTER 5
An Axolotl 79

CHAPTER 6
Another New Key 97

CHAPTER 7
An Interview with Aisopos 113

CHAPTER 8
No More Coincidences 127

CHAPTER 9
Jagged Edges 143

CHAPTER 10
Signs 157

CHAPTER 11
When All That Remains Is Dust
and Dust Will Never Truly Leave Anyway 171

CHAPTER 12
The Winner 183

EPILOGUE
Aisopos Tells Us Everything 195

Acknowledgements 209

CHAPTER 1

The Arrival

What would you do if a three-and-a-half-pawed, no-eyed cat with a bloody squirrel's tail hanging from its mouth turned up at your apartment one day, and when you opened the door it dropped the tail at your feet and scooted between your legs and over to your wool sweater—the corn-like one with a ring of grey triangles around the middle that was knit special for you by the shopkeeper of the hardware store down the street, because of all of the business you'd provided her over the years in the form of key-cutting—and began pulling up the fibres with the real claws of one paw and the imaginary claws of the other, until it decided the garment was good enough for lying down upon, and curled itself into a circle, and didn't close its eyes, because it couldn't, and gave its own tail a few rough licks, and then, presumably, fell asleep?

I named him Scoot.

As Scoot presumably slept, I bent closer to examine the scabs where patches of his orange fur were missing and discovered him to be riddled with juicy brown lice. Foraging in his ears, his cheeks and neck, they traversed his spine, rendezvousing in the hip and back leg area as though it were a truck stop, before carrying on toward his lower belly. I poked him with a hockey stick. Nothing happened. Then I reached the hockey stick out to close the door and watched as the door dragged the squirrel's tail along with it, wedging it against the frame, so it was half inside, half out of the apartment. That was also when I noticed a sock ball that'd been stranded behind the door for who knows how long; I hooked it over to myself and shot it at the wall.

It happened to my friend Sarah once, too. She woke up one January morning to a fishbowl waiting at her front door. The water was cold and the fish inside was almost dead, so she brought it in, cleared a space on top of her dresser and turned up the heat. Within minutes the fish began to come back to life. She said it didn't swim, it danced jetés at the surface of the water, which made her imagine walking into the room one day to find the fish flopping on the floor. The thought of which, she said, made her want to puke. But whether or not she wanted to, over the next few days Sarah collected plants and a small castle to place inside the bowl to help the fish feel properly adopted. It worked. She said that in the mornings it would come to the front of the bowl and wag its fins like a dog's tail. She said the fish was basically a dog. I can confirm that I did witness first-hand the fish wag its fins like a dog's tail, when Sarah was out of town one night and needed me to go over and feed it.

During the three and a half years the fish lived on Sarah's dresser, Sarah quit two jobs, including cashier at a boutique stationery store and cashier at a boutique terrarium store, and was fired from a third when she was caught stealing a container of four-dollar-and-ninety-five-cent fish food as a stock clerk at Walmart. She also established and sang lead in two bands that played a total of two shows each, and had one abortion, which coincided with the suicide of the boyfriend she'd been dating for one month. That was when I came to feed the fish, while she was away at the funeral.

The point is, when we buried the fish in a tissue box in the vacant lot beside Sarah's house that we called the backyard, Sarah cried in a way I'd never seen. Or heard, I should say. Because her face was pressed against my chest for the entire duration of the spell. It was a weeping. It made me cry, too. But it also made the ground, fence, sky and breeze all disappear, so in the end it was just us, amidst all that water. In that moment, I wondered if things might be different if she still worked at Walmart. Or was still dating her dead boyfriend. Probably not. Because if not those, it would be other things.

Which is why Sarah was the person I called after I'd knocked over the lamp from the nightstand with the sock ball and Scoot still didn't wake up.

"Austin?" she said. "I don't believe you."

"That's a really nice way to talk to your friend."

"It's just sleeping right now?"

"I've been as destructive as is appropriate within my own home. He won't wake up."

*

Approximately thirty-five minutes later, Sarah arrived at the door to find the then bent-in-half squirrel's tail folded at the threshold in front of her feet. She was carrying a small plastic bag from the pharmacy.

"Shampoo," she said. "And a little present to say welcome home."

She stepped over the tail to where Scoot was sleeping.

"You didn't tell me it had no eyes," she said, looking down at him.

"I forgot because he was sleeping anyway."

"Right."

She dumped the contents of the pharmacy bag onto my bed, then fit the bag over her hand like a glove and used it to pick up the squirrel's tail. She carried it past me and through the kitchenette, where she tossed it out the hole in the broken windowpane above the sink onto the street below.

"That's gross," she said.

I balanced myself with the hockey stick as I crouched down to my toes to dangle the fake mouse toy she'd brought in front of Scoot's face. Lice crawled over his furry sockets, down the bridge of his nose, to the spots where his whiskers sprouted from. His whiskers didn't twitch.

"He's sleeping like he's never slept in his life," I said. "This is sleep number one."

"It's clearly unbelievably happy. Inconceivably happy," said Sarah.

I knew then, after Sarah had said inconceivably, that whether or not I wanted it, I had a responsibility to now make Scoot feel properly adopted, just as she had the fish. She took the hockey stick from my grip and I fell backwards, having lost my balance. She slid the blade beneath Scoot's chin and gently lifted it, then dropped it back down. Then did that again, and then tried wedging it under his belly until finally he released a purr, rolled onto his back and stretched his whole body out like a snake. He looked like he only weighed about as much as a snake, too; he was so skinny and long. Patches of pink belly skin were exposed where lice nibbled at his nipples.

"It's moving, but I don't know if it's awake because of its eyes," said Sarah.

"Scoot," I said.

"You named it?"

"Wake up, Scoot. It's time for your bath."

THE ARRIVAL

"I think Scoot is a good name."

I looked up at her. She looked nice that day in her black tights and purple skirt and white puff jacket with her several beaded bracelets that produced a calming rattle.

"I think so, too," I said.

"Maybe just pick it up and take it to the shower. But scoop it in the sweater, so you don't get lice all over yourself."

Sarah was smart. I needed her. I swaddled Scoot in the sweater and held him in a cradled position, still not sure if he was awake or asleep. Either way, he didn't resist being held. His one and a half front paws hung limply above his face and bounced with each step I took toward the washroom. I also needed Sarah to pull back the shower curtain and turn on the taps.

He stood upright in the stall while I shampooed his patches of fur and exposed skin, then settled afterward in my lap like it was a chair as I sat on the washroom floor and combed the lice from his fur.

"I feel like they're on me," said Sarah, as she scratched her scalp and pulled her hands inside of her sleeves to scratch her arms, then wormed her hands down the waistband of her tights to her thighs. "What a terrible feeling. How is it so seemingly unfazed?"

"It's like they're his remoras."

"You're sure it's a male?"

I shifted around to display Scoot's genitalia to her.

"Do you see that thing?" I said, combing a louse from the fur below his testicles. "That's it right there. A cat penis."

Sarah scratched at her cheeks, her neck and behind her ears, leaving red lines all over herself.

"What do you have to do today?" I asked her.

"A parcel pickup and fertilize the orchid. But I've already finished those tasks."

A parcel pickup meant Sarah had to go all the way down to the shipping docks for her landlord, Aisopos, to gather a parcel that arrived by boat from Greece approximately once every three weeks. We didn't know what the parcels contained, or who sent them, but we knew that they were ten by fourteen by four inches, and a little but not really all that heavy. We also didn't know why they were addressed to the outlet at the docks and not Aisopos's house. But the reason we didn't know those things was because when Sarah asked, he pretended not to speak English anymore. And the reason Sarah was the one who picked them up and not Aisopos was that Aisopos was ninety years old and used a wheelchair, and it was agreed upon verbally in advance that as long as Sarah helped him out with a few, at the time, non-specified tasks, she could have twenty dollars deducted from her rent each month.

"He can't fertilize the orchid?" I asked her.

"His hands shake too much. And I like to do it anyway. It's one of my favourite things."

"Most of the things you do are your favourite things. I'd say you are a successful person."

"I know that at least I'm not depressed," she said.

Scoot was becoming restless sitting on my lap. Before letting him go, I bent over top of him and kissed a bald spot on the crown of his head. His one and a half paws twitched in a kneading motion, then he hopped off my lap and scooted around Sarah's legs, through the door, and out to the centre of the room, where he sat very still, air drying.

"I'd say he's looking much less full of bugs," I said.

"I'll go shopping with you now," said Sarah.

"Go?"

"For supplies."

I thought about the hole in the kitchenette window.

"What if he escapes through that hole?"

"Cover it up."

I tried to think of something that could be used to cover it up, but all I could come up with was cardboard, of which I had none of any sort.

"What if one of us does the shopping while the other stays here to guard the hole?" I said.

Sarah paused her scratching and moved to the side so I could have a clear view of Scoot sitting in the exact same position he was in prior to all this shopping talk. He might have even fallen back to sleep. There really was no way of telling.

"I think if there was ever a time to go, it would be now," said Sarah.

I reminded myself that I had chosen for Sarah to be here today for a reason, being that she was a person I could trust in this situation. As far as I was aware, at least in the time I had known her, which was nearly seven years, Sarah had never made a decision that resulted in the endangerment of the life of another living creature, if you don't count the abortion, which I don't, or the death of her ex-boyfriend, which I've often needed to remind her to not count herself.

So I got up from the washroom floor, shook the sweater over the drain and ran the water to rinse away the fallen lice. My shirt was wet and so were the crotch and thighs of my pants. I walked past Sarah and surveyed the perimeter of my apartment, which was only a two-hundred-square-foot room, so really I just turned in a circle looking for any possible materials Scoot could potentially use to construct a device to turn a doorknob. He got up here, after all. And the building's entrance was steel and locked with an iron bolt that weighed at least five pounds, as well as a padlock, and the elevator operated by crank.

"He'll be here," she said.

I laid the sweater back down on the floor and bunched up the sleeves in an attempt to recreate Scoot's heap for him. Then I fished the sock ball out from behind the bed and pulled it apart so as to pull those socks over my feet.

"I am putting on my socks and shoes because I trust you," I said to Sarah as she stuffed the hole in the window with my only pillow.

"Thank you," she said. "And I'm sorry I didn't say that to you earlier when I spoke to you over the phone."

*

From the entrance, it was a four-minute walk to the pet section—the very last section in a back corner of the store where even the music didn't reach. The speakers ended at the lawn furniture. Above, the overhead lights had burned out. I asked Sarah if it felt weird going shopping at the Walmart she'd been fired from.

"I come here all the time and I don't care," she said. "What would you do if you had to go to Walmart?"

She made a good point; I'd probably go to Walmart. The good thing, anyway, was that pushing a shopping cart was preventing her from scratching. She had really done a number on herself. Soft red scabs bubbled over two moles on her neck.

"It's always been this way," she whispered as we turned into the first of its two aisles. "Go to the end and look."

She pointed her chin ahead of us. While she waited back, I walked forward, slowly, turning two or three times to look over my shoulder at her, because she was making a very serious but also cheeky face, and I was realizing then just how much Sarah reminded me of Judge Judy. At the end of the aisle, I peeked around the corner. A white-haired man in a red kaftan dress was seated atop a stack of large dog food bags, seemingly engrossed in a paperback novel.

I turned and walked back toward Sarah very quickly, not checking over my shoulder in the other direction this time, because I didn't want to see if he should suddenly appear behind me.

"He lives here," she whispered. "But no one believes me."

I looked to the ceiling.

"There are no cameras," she said. "Not even mirrors. They stop at the fishing equipment. That's how I know he's to blame. He told them. How else could they have caught me?"

"That was months ago," I said.

"I know, but still."

"Why would he deliberately draw attention to himself, if you are in fact right about him living here?"

"I am right, and to hoodwink them."

I was feeling very disturbed and wanted to get out of Walmart as soon as possible. I grabbed the closest bag of kibble, which had a picture of a cougar on it, and dropped it into the cart.

"Let's go," I said.

But Sarah didn't go. She took the bag from the cart and held it up to check the expiry date, then swapped it for another from the back of the shelf. She bumped the cart forward and into my hip.

"Ow," I said.

"Litter and a litter tray. And treats."

*

Leaving Walmart, Sarah outlined a verbal map of the city to demonstrate how she'd walked three quarters of it in the span of that single Tuesday morning.

"You made a really good choice in food for Scoot," she also said. "You're a natural cat dad."

I couldn't believe how stressful it was being a dad. In a way, I was happier feeling disturbed by the kaftan man, because at least then I wasn't thinking up ways that Scoot could potentially depress the lever of the toaster with his tail drooped inside of it. If Sarah hadn't been with me and had the two bags I was carrying not been just awkwardly shaped and disproportionately weighted enough to prevent me from doing so, I probably would have sprinted the twelve blocks back to my apartment. But she was there. And the bags were as they were. And I suppose you don't always want to appear on the outside like how your thoughts appear on the inside.

Which is all to say that once I saw the rusting green roof of the former mops, brushes and brooms factory where I now lived, I removed the key from my pocket in such haste that I dropped the bag with the litter tray and treats in it to the ground, where it was caught by the wind and nearly blew out onto the street. So Sarah was able to see the truth of it, a bit. Regardless, I think she, too, was anxious to reconfirm Scoot's existence within my apartment, because she just ran after the bag and saved it, then kept onward a pace ahead of me without even so much as a Judge Judy–like facial remark until we'd rounded the corner into the alley and stood facing the steel door outside.

"Thanks for that," I said to her as she took the other bag from my hand so I could handle the padlock. "I wasn't thinking. Putting all the light items together in one bag, and all the heavy ones together in the other like that. I just didn't think."

"We all mismanage our bagging sometimes. What's wrong?"

I forced against the key. Nothing happened.

"Not turning," I said.

Sarah set the bags on the ground and tapped my shoulder. I moved to the side and listened to the sounds I could hear in that moment that didn't actually exist, sort of like three skillets falling from an overhead rack that'd snapped off at one end and were landing on top of a cat in quick succession. She stepped away from the lock, the key still jammed, and I could tell she was hearing something, too. I forced a smile.

"Hah," I said.

"You don't have to do that."

I jiggled the key loose from the lock and squeezed it in both hands, which I held up at my lips and nostrils in a prayer position. I closed my eyes, entreating to the now damp, tangy-smelling brass. Then I stuck it back into the padlock. It turned.

"Fuck," I said, relieved.

Sarah bent to lift the bolt and I pulled the door open, and both of us practically ran through the hallway to the elevator, grabbing hold of the lever at the same time to turn the crank. By that point, the sounds had evolved into a painful buzzing and snapping, like a patch cord plugged into an amp being chewed on. Then, as we watched the elevator slowly appear from above, total silence. Like carbon monoxide drifting through vents.

But after towing the elevator up the shaft, pushing back its screen and unlocking the door to the space that was once the office of the former factory, and was now my current home, we found him, Scoot, on the foot of the bed, perched like a three-and-a-half-pawed, no-eyed sphinx, and I fell to my knees beside the mattress.

"We got you food," I said. "We got you litter, and a litter tray to use."

Scoot yawned and stretched his arm to my shoulder. A louse crawled from his paw and onto my shirt. Right then, the only instinct I had was to offer him a treat. Just for being there, like a good boy. So I went to fetch the treats from the bags that I realized we'd left outside.

"You're crying," said Sarah.

I wiped a drip from my nose.

"We left the bags in the alley," I said.

"Look here," she said.

She pointed to her right eye where a tear was dangling off the shelf of her bottom lid. I smiled, because as that tear fell, the noise officially ended. Sarah's right eye certainly had a way with things. Things meaning me. Which is also why, three weeks later, on a much more winter-like winter's day, after I'd wrapped Scoot in his sweater and carried him four blocks in a milk crate to the nearest vet, Sarah was the first person I called.

"I need you," I said to her.

"Okay," she replied, and somehow was standing next to me, my hand held in both of hers, before Scoot had even been called into the examination room.

*

In the parkette across the street from the vet there was a bench. I sat on it. Sarah stood facing me, doing leg lifts to keep warm. It was all grey, sky and ground, and snowing sharp snowflakes. I watched them dot the rim of the milk crate.

The second person I called was Dan.

"Scoot's gone," I said into the phone.

"Got out?"

"No."

There was a long interval during which I let the phone slide down to my cheek. Sarah paused her leg lifts and lifted my elbow so it went back up to my ear.

"The options were limited."

"You don't adopt pets you can't afford the vet bills for," he said.

I moaned like I had a swimming cramp, because that's what it felt like inside. Like I was swimming in a lake in the woods in the middle of December with all my clothes on, in a dream, and I couldn't move fast enough to get to shore before death took over. I hung up. Then I called Brad.

"She said she believes it to be feline infectious peritonitis, caused by a mutant strain of a feline coronavirus. She's never seen it before. Never had seen it. Believed. She was making an educated guess."

"Austin? Is that you?"

"But we don't know where, or when, he would have contracted the virus. You can see my name on your phone."

"Where are you?"

"Bernadette Parkette. I'm with Sarah and a milk crate."

"You talking about that thing?"

"Scoot?"

"Yeah."

"Yes."

"Okay, so you're at the vet? What's she look like?"

I hung up. Called Kirk.

"He got so skinny so fast."

Then I called Gunner.

"So, he's gone."

And then, finally, there, in the cold lake, out of breath, with a cramp, shivering, turning blue, treading water in heavy jeans, I stopped thinking about my brothers.

"Hello?" said Gunner.

Sarah took the phone from me and hung up.

"Is there anyone else you would like to call?" she said.

As I began to die, the milk crate waiting on the frozen sand off the shore began to float up into the sky.

"What more is there to say?"

*

Walking home, I supposed that I could remove the skillets from beneath the bed and hang them back up on the rack. I could take the patch cord out from underneath the stack of T-shirts in the cupboard where I kept T-shirts and I could unpin the towel pinned over the vent and use it again for drying my body when it was wet. I didn't need to carry the milk crate in a hug anymore. I let it fall in only one hand and walked with it bumping against the outside of my thigh instead.

Sarah split up with me halfway back to my home in order to go in the direction of hers. She had spent so much time being cold for me that day, I thought I would soon take her to the Holiday Inn to use the hot tub as a way to say thank you. By the time I reached the laneway that led to the building, Scoot's sweater that used to be my sweater, and I guessed could be again, if I washed it, had fallen three quarters of the way out of the milk crate. The sleeve was dragging on the ground. I dumped it all the way out and stood on top of it and closed my eyes and imagined I was asleep. Then I opened my eyes, lifted the bolt and wedged the key into the padlock, where it snapped.

THE ARRIVAL

*

So what would you do if you were stuck outside your building with half a key in the palm of your hand, and your phone started vibrating because your ex-best friend Hadir had sent you a photo of a painting that was taken in Japan of a three-and-a-half-pawed, no-eyed cat with orange fur, perched in a sphinx position on the edge of a table, and you couldn't tell if the cat was sleeping or awake, and across the top of the painting were words painted in Japanese that you couldn't understand, but across the bottom were words in English that you could and they read, *Much reward*, and beneath the image was the message, *Isn't this your weird cat? haha looks just like her.* And you closed the message to open the photo you took of your cat back when he was alive, in the morning, perched as he most liked to be, like a sphinx, on the foot of your bed, just mere minutes before you scooped him into a milk crate, and you realized that the subject of the painting was, in fact, an exact replica of the subject of your own photo?

    The Holiday Inn would have to wait.

CHAPTER 2

A New Key

"I saw you and your girlfriend walking."

Grear spun her ring of many keys to find the spare of mine she'd cut for herself after my fourth visit in three weeks, two years ago. I placed the half key on the counter and she slid it right off the edge into the trash bin.

"Grear, what do you know about Japan?" I asked her.

"What part of it?"

"The whole country, and better still, its contemporary art movement."

"Well." She spoke slowly. "What I know's that it's got one of the lowest homicide rates in the world. Does that help your question?"

Grear was in her seventies and from Scotland. So she could be considered to be wise. I thought about the possible connection that might exist between art and murder in Japan.

"Perhaps in Japanese culture, those with a desire to inflict death upon others are taught to redirect their impulses toward creative pursuits," I said. "I wonder if the artist I'm thinking of has any experience with this sort of moral edification or not. Maybe I could find an interview with them online."

I took out my phone and reopened Hadir's message. There was no signature on the painting, but a comment below the image read *#BadDogBadArt*. I typed this into a search bar and waited for something to happen while Grear cut my new key.

"Is your Wi-Fi working, Grear?" I asked when nothing continued to happen.

"Not yet. But thank you for reminding me."

She wrote a note to herself on the palm of her hand, the fourth note in the past three months that I'd reminded her to write, to *Call the guy*, and showed it to me with a wink. On the television behind her, Eva Price was wearing a reindeer costume that made it next to impossible not to acknowledge her voluminous thighs. Grear indicated behind the counter to the removable seat row from a van.

"You come and sit?" she said. "I think Adam's finally going to make his move."

"Thanks, Grear, but I really have to get to Wi-Fi."

She placed the new key on the counter and pulled from her hair a pencil, along with a small pin I could use to extract the other half of the key from the lock. She tapped the pencil against the counter three times.

"Add it to my tab," I said. "Any news on Anna?"

"Caught out in a car park trying to flee to Scotland," she said.

"How?"

"Phelan. She'd gone snooping in his office, you know, looking for evidence. Eileen comes walking through the door, Anna goes and whacks the poor woman unconscious thinking it was him. Spooked-like."

A NEW KEY

I must have come across indifferent after hearing the news about Anna, even though it wasn't really much of a surprise, considering a person could only be on the run for so long after escaping prison via the hospital after having had a mental breakdown in their cell, because Grear asked me if I'd already seen what happens next.

"It's just been a weird day. Sarah is my friend still."

Grear pencilled the key into the carbon copy book next to the calculator next to the cash box, then reached below the counter to procure a package of instant ramen.

"One day," she said, holding it out to me.

"Real life isn't like how it is on *Coronation Street*, Grear," I said, slipping the fresh key and hair pin into the breast pocket of my jacket, and the noodles into the pocket that formed between my shirt and the waistband of my jacket. "Except sometimes, when it kind of is."

*

Inside the apartment, I dropped the sweater, wet from having been left on the ground, as well as the milk crate and the package of ramen, to the floor. In the way I'd become accustomed to, in order to hear the vibrations of Scoot's purring, I knelt in front of the bed. But instead of pressing my ear to the mattress, I placed my phone where my ear would go. I connected to "Ronda," an unprotected network somewhere in the building that was in close enough vicinity to offer a bar of its fan, and refreshed the search result for *#BadDogBadArt*. Some cutesy images of dogs, real and renderings, appeared, as well as a list of links. I tapped the first and found myself in an online shop from Colorado selling mostly ornamental quotes that would only appeal to dog owners, such as,

In times of darkness, glimpse the soul of a dog and you'll no longer wonder if there is not pure goodness in this world still, and *I don't need therapy, I just need a dog.* I clicked the latter and was subsequently taken to an option to purchase the quote printed onto a mug, a wooden placard or a canvas tote bag. I selected the bag, then was taken to another option to purchase either a beige bag with black print, or a black bag with white print. Again, I chose the latter, and watched as the shopping cart icon in the top right corner of my phone instantly transformed into a red number one. I closed the web page, opened a fresh search bar and typed in the comment again, this time adding *japan* at the end of it.

The next set of images to appear were much more ominous than those generated by the first search result. For instance, instead of a relatively charming painting of a French bulldog with a cigarette dangling from the corner of its mouth, or a realistic pencil sketch of a proud-looking greyhound, there was a medieval etching of a mutt walking upright on its hind legs, ribs protruded, eyes drawn in a red pigment, its triangular teeth bared. Another image looked more like a wolf than a dog, again, with red eyes and also red highlights interspersed throughout its fur. I tapped the first link below the wolf dog and was redirected to an article published in *Japan Views Lifestyle News in English* about an installation piece that featured everyday items, chewed, lacquered and mounted onto the closed shutters of an out-of-business tofu shop in the Taitō Ward of Tokyo. The author noted how the piece was bringing an influx of local tourism to the area, providing nearby businesses with surplus business, and also posed the question to the artist: *Why do you think this work has resonated so much with both aesthetes and members of the general public of Tokyo alike?*

Ahead of the response, a split image of the mural and the artist had been interpolated into the text. I brought the phone closer to my face, then zoomed in and scrolled my way from right to left, examining the flip-flop-style slippers, unfolded fans, purses, belts, watchbands, bras, once-beautiful fabrics that could have been anything from kimonos to curtains, magazines, book covers, musical notation, perhaps, toothbrushes and the thick, criss-crossing streaks of paint that looked like the muddied, purplish-greyish colour that water turns after a brush has been rinsed in it several times, until I was face to face with BadDog himself. His hair, black and grey and white, reached past his shoulders. His facial hair was ungroomed, also long and mostly white, and his skin would make it seem as though he'd spent most of his life outdoors. But the most striking aspect of BadDog's appearance was his smile, which you would maybe not even recognize as a smile unless you were zoomed in to the maximum point possible right at the place where mouth meets cheek. But there it was, extending just past the overhang of his moustache hair. A perfect right angle at the juncture of his two lips.

I zoomed back out as quickly as possible. I was nervous to continue reading, to know the murderous intentions behind the creation of a man like this. Who, or what, could drive a person to chew up the nipple of a baby bottle? Or a Hello Kitty thong? How psychotic do you need to be to create an entire nine-foot-wide mural in the first place?

I set the phone down on the bed and let the screen go black. A gust of wind beat against the pillow in the window, and the copper pipe that ran along the perimeter of the kitchenette ceiling rattled. If you had asked me prior to three weeks ago if the rattling pipes in my apartment bothered me, I would have said, "What pipes?" But having since observed the twitches of Scoot's ears at the slightest of each tinny knock, I'd become all too aware of them: the double row of black iron above the bed, the vertical drain stack beside the front door. In fact, I'd started to wonder if I'd ever noticed anything about my surroundings before Scoot had showed me how he listened to them.

I woke up the phone.

BadDog's response to the author's question, which the author had translated from Japanese to English, read as follows:

The piece acts as a mirror that reflects to the beholder their own suppressed inner nature. From the moment we gain the capability to do so, our mothers and fathers tell us not to run and not to howl. Our teachers tell us not to hit and bite. Everyone—our bosses, doctors, government officials, officers of the law—tells us that if we chew things other than food, use our claws to shred consumer goods or otherwise, there will be severe consequences. Our livelihoods will be at stake. However, just because this is the predominant code of ethics in our society does not mean that the animal inside of us does not continue to live. In fact, being told "no" as much as we are told it only makes us more ravenous. That is what the people are seeing—their misunderstood, belittled, profoundly ravenous hunger.

I was suddenly disconnected from Ronda. I looked up from the screen to the aluminum air duct above the front door that sounded like a microwave popping popcorn, then to the package of ramen on the floor, in front of the door. Was I hungry? Kind of. But even if I still had a microwave with which to cook said ramen noodles in a relative instant, would I still be hungry after eating them? Enough to chew up a bar of deodorant, or a plastic poinsettia? Or go out and murder somebody? Is murder-hunger a hunger you even feel with your stomach?

A NEW KEY

I checked the time on my phone. It was shortly after seven, so it made sense that everything around me was so dark. I stood from my knees to put back on the shoes that I realized I'd never taken off in the first place, and, as well, the jacket that I was still wearing, with the new key still tucked in its breast pocket. As if I'd known I would soon need to be so, I was already ready to go to the library.

*

It was a short walk, less than ten minutes, even, to the nearest one, but I still encountered a person wearing a silver bodysuit prancing along the side of the road spinning light-up devil sticks in that time. Prior to the article from *Japan Views Lifestyle News in English*, I would have just thought to myself, *Here's a guy practising a thing he likes to do*. But now, I couldn't help but wonder how pervasive BadDog's animalistic philosophy might actually be. Did it extend beyond the realm of contemporary Japanese art, beyond even the borders of Japan itself? Could BadDog be influencing people engaged in all sorts of hobbies and trades, in this country and probably others too? How were these people, or animals, connected to Scoot? Was there a rogue member close by involved in the intercontinental theft and delivery of a deformed, or possibly mutilated cat to my door? Where did the art begin, and life end? And what was the much reward being offered for his impossible return?

I followed the classical guitar coming from the small speaker tucked in the side pocket of a man's purple plastic backpack up the switchbacks of the library entrance ramp. Inside, the only computer available was next to a girl with blue hair and blue eyeshadow and black lipstick and a lip ring. It seemed, at that point, that anyone in the neighbourhood could have been the one who was either ferrying a feline message to me or setting me up to be framed in what was turning out to be, so far, a lethal situation. I pulled out the chair and sat down.

"Hi," I said to the girl.

Though she didn't respond, she turned her face halfway towards mine until she was looking somewhere in the space between our two screens. So I talked to her some more.

"My adopted pet cat died today," I said. "Through no fault of my own."

She nodded yes, like she already knew.

"How's your day going?" I asked her.

She turned her face back to her own screen. I leaned over to see what she was composing in her Word document.

"Essay?" I said.

She looked down at her keyboard and started typing with her index and middle fingers. I watched as the words appeared above.

It's for my history teacher. Ha ha.

"Hah," I said, scanning the first paragraph. *Canada's role in World War Two.* "Good one."

Thanks, she typed, then continued typing something else. *What's your homework?*

"Art. Contemporary. Social Studies. Geography."

Sucks, ha ha.

"Ya, it both sucks and is funny." I entered *#BadDogBadArt japan* into the search bar and opened the link to the article again. "Have you heard of this artist in Japan?"

She looked between our screens again. *No*, she typed.

"Do you like animals?" I asked.

Ya but I'm allergic to everything ha ha.

She hit the backspace button repeatedly, deleting each letter of her end of our conversation, then dropped a textbook onto the keyboard and began flipping the pages, one at a time, while sighing, for many chapters. It seemed like she really was a teenager who had homework to do.

I scrolled past BadDog's comment and continued reading the article. What followed was information regarding a certain art contest into which BadDog himself had entered and found himself as one of ten finalists. Could I, as a loyal reader of *Japan Views Lifestyle News in English*, please take a moment, then, to follow the following link and cast my vote for BadDog? The winner stood to acquire twenty-five thousand yen in prize money, as well as the opportunity to take part in a group exhibition at Hōnto No Kimochi Gallery and Café in Setagaya City, Tokyo, Japan.

I opened a new search page and typed: *how many canadian dollars is equal to 25000 yen?* At that moment in time, the answer was two hundred and eighty-five dollars and forty-three cents. I went back to the article and clicked the link to the contest page. Below the name of each finalist was a short biographical statement, including BadDog's: *BadDog is a painter, sculptor, installation artist. You find his work around and in the street, if you look for it.* What? Around where? There was no website. What street? I sent all the information regarding the contest, including the other nine artist biographies, to the printer, as well as the original article. Then I stood, tucked the chair back into place and was about to leave when the girl reached over and tugged on my sleeve. She pointed at her computer screen.

High school is bs. Ha ha.

"You could drop out and become a comedian," I said, to which she nodded yes again, like she'd been trying to tell her parents that forever.

*

Back at the apartment, with my new key, latte and fifteen printed sheets of reading material, I pulled the barber stool, found two years prior in the laneway adjacent to the laneway leading to the entrance of the former factory where I now lived, up to the one-by-one-foot countertop space beside the single stovetop in the kitchenette and began to read.

There were no other streets mentioned in the remaining biographies—only names, the names of post-secondary institutions in Japan, the names of some earthquakes and tsunamis, and the ways in which several sets of parents died, including during, and after, earthquakes and tsunamis. At the end of the list was a note about the deadline to vote in the contest: *December 20, 23:59*. I took my phone from my pocket and connected to Ronda and searched: *what is the time difference between here and japan?* Twelve hours. Then I checked the date and time of my current location. December 19, 8:35 pm EST. Or, 20:35. So it was already 09:35, deadline day, in Tokyo. Below the words *Click Here to Vote* was a telephone number and address for the café and gallery in Setagaya City. I searched the name of the street and a map with a red pin appeared, as well as the website for the contest again.

Sirens sounded somewhere not far from where I lived. After they'd ended, some more sounded. It was a freaking loop, all of it. And somehow, I'd ended up inside. But would it end once the contest did? Or only if BadDog won? Could I convince BadDog that it wasn't my fault Scoot had died? Unless, was it? I looked at the wall in front of me, then at the one adjacent to that, both dotted with black stains in the corners. Had I not provided a habitable enough habitat to prevent a small, and likely easily susceptible creature, due to his deformities, from getting sick?

*

That night, as Ronda cut in and out, I spent one hour and twenty-five minutes watching one twenty-three-minute episode of *Judge Judy* on my phone, while eating some, but not all, of Grear's ramen noodles from a skillet of hot water. Eventually, I tried to sleep. But something, either the latte or the blue light exposure or the many different percussive pitches emanating from the pipes like a drum line or the sirens averaging at around twelve-minute intervals, if I had to guess, or the fact that I was still fully dressed, wearing shoes, and lying on top of the sheets, or the lack of pillow, was keeping me awake. And also, after twenty-one nights of having one paw rhythmically knead my shin bone while the stub where the other paw would be, if it existed, twitched like a heartbeat against my calf as a gentle reminder to not move, not even a quarter of a quarter of an inch, lest I disturb the precious body attached to those paws resting alongside myself at the foot of the bed, I was now alone. There were no longer any boundaries forcing me to rest.

So I sat up. Phone already in hand, I reopened the message from Hadir to more closely examine the picture of the painting. There was no denying it—there he was. The cat who would become the cat named Scoot, perched next to an orange cup with a square handle, atop a greyish-brownish circular table likely made of wood, in a room also brownish in colour, and with a curtain-less window on the right side of the wall, through which the black shadow of a person outside, and possibly looking in, could be seen. I looked away from the phone to the real window above the real sink in my own apartment, briefly, double-checking for a shadowed figure I knew couldn't be there. Then back to the picture. Beyond the edges of the painting was the outline of a whitish-brownish base, presumably a tabletop of some sort, and also, in all probability, made of wood. At the bottom right corner of that wood was a crescent stain, the likes of which were commonly produced from the bottoms of wet cups. The painting had been set on a table and photographed. I looked at the username above the image: @tacka_attack_love.

Who was Tacka Attack Love?

I closed the picture, then downloaded the Instagram app onto my phone. Upon prompting me for a username, I entered @Austinsusername. When it asked me to upload a photo for my profile, I took a photo of the space in front of me, in the dark, and used that. When it finally stopped bugging me, I found the option to search.

Tacka Attack Love was a young woman from Fukuoka prefecture. She had wavy brown bangs, a chunk of quartz in the palm of her hand, two friends with whom she liked to sip drinks through straws, and headphones that looked like turtle shells. Most importantly, she had a painting of Scoot, right there, in the place of the fifth-most-recent post on her Instagram account. I tapped the photo to enlarge it. It had been liked two times, once each by @maki18892 and @rockparty. Below, Tacka had commented #BadDogBadArt. Tapping that comment subsequently transported me to a group of fifteen photos, three of which were paintings, including Tacka's painting of Scoot, one of a sculpture that looked like golden poo, and eleven of the murals featured in *Japan Views Lifestyle News in English*, taken at different angles, in different lights, and occasionally with a different person standing in front of it flashing the peace sign.

I went back to the account of Tacka Attack Love and scrolled further down her page. It was clear she enjoyed going to the same beach over and over again and taking pictures of her feet in the water there. It was also clear she didn't like her own face, because in every photo of herself she'd either turned her head to the side or tilted it toward her chest so that it was never actually visible. I closed the app and searched: *fukuoka prefecture beach*. Again, a map with a red pin appeared. I zoomed out. The beach was 197 hours away from Tokyo by foot. Around what street did Tacka find Bad-Dog's portrait of Scoot? And why did she want it, even?

What was she hiding by hiding her face?

What was Ronda hiding by cutting out, once again, at the exact moment that I needed to tap the word *Follow*?

*

When 06:00 EST arrived, I packed the pillowcase that had been laying empty on my bed since the day the pillow it was supposed to cover was lodged into the window hole, with my fifteen papers, new key, and phone, and carried everything out with me into the very dark, very snowy morning.

I never understood exactly where Hadir's parents' house was; I just took the streetcar I knew went there and rode it east as far as it would go. When it reached the end of the tracks, I knew then to keep walking until I passed the second Bangladeshi restaurant and market, the one by the Dairy Queen, and then to cross the street to the north side, turn left and walk straight until I saw the one-storey house with the blue awning pulled out, because it was stuck that way, above their concrete porch. By the time I'd reached it that day, you'd think the sun would have been coming up. But it wasn't yet. There was one light on in the den.

Hadir lived underground in the lower part of the house. He almost never came up any higher because he played video games. I dug away the snow that had piled up in front of his window to see his headphone-swaddled profile lit by the white glow of the computer screen in the dark room below. Then I knocked on the window. I knocked again, harder. I knocked a lot, with both hands, because of Hadir's headphones. Eventually, he looked up, and when he did, he spilled the teacup of Sour Patch Kids he was holding in his lap, as though he were surprised to see me there, and made a signal with both hands.

"What does that mean?" I said, even though he couldn't hear me.

He did it again, exasperated.

"You're exasperated?" I said. Then I made a similar, albeit more sloppy set of hand signals, since I was holding a pillowcase, back at him. "You figure that out, major general."

After that, I could tell Hadir had become very frustrated, because he turned back to his computer, typed something short, then clicked the mouse with excess force. Then, he removed his headphones and hung them over the monitor, also with a lot of force, pushed his chair to the window, forcefully flipped up the latch to unlock it and pushed open the pane.

"What the hell is wrong with you, you sick fucking skeever? It's the middle of the night and you're looking at me through a window? What's with the thing?"

He grabbed at the end of my pillowcase.

"He was a he," I said.

"What?"

"Scoot. He." I pulled the pillowcase out from his grip, then stood back up. "And it's almost 07:30 Eastern Standard Time. Most people in this time zone are waking up now. And in a lot of the other ones, they're already out doing things like awaiting the results of major contests."

"Who the fuck is Scoot?"

I didn't bother to answer the question. I was already walking away from Hadir's parents' house at that point, and I wasn't going to stop, except for one moment, only, when I reached the sidewalk and heard my name as it was called out from the porch.

"Austin?"

Hadir's dad was standing outside wearing nothing but winter boots and a brown robe tied loosely over his belly. I didn't yell anything back, just gave him a thumbs up to confirm that it was, in fact, me, Austin. Because I had nothing to hide. Quite the contrary, actually. I had a lot of things to find. Starting with the directions to, and between, multiple places within Japan.

I slung the pillowcase over my shoulder. A siren wailed past the end of the street.

CHAPTER 3

Gross Garbage
All Over the Ground

Not all the lights had been switched on in the library yet, and despite it being a new day, it still wasn't not dark outside the windows, so the map of Tokyo on the computer screen in front of me was like a big, bright spotlight I had to look slightly to the right of. From the pillowcase, I pulled the paper with the address of Hōnto No Kimochi Gallery and Café and typed it into the search bar beside the map, which automatically zoomed in on a block surrounding a red pin. Next, I took out the article from *Japan Views Lifestyle News in English* and typed in the name of the street where BadDog had installed his mural. The map then dilated to show a three-hour-and-twenty-six-minute walking route of blue dots that crested through the city in a wavy line. I clicked *print* from the drop-down menu. Then I clicked my way back from the view of Tokyo, all the way back until the entire country of Japan was apparent, as well as North Korea, South Korea, a whole bunch of China and some of Russia. For a second, I was an astronaut. I even lifted my feet off the floor.

"I do that too, sometimes."

A library clerk pushed a cart behind me. She smiled at me like she thought I needed her to.

"I'm okay," I said.

"It's okay," she said, still walking. "I'm not judging. Like I said, I sit in that exact spot, and do that exact same thing sometimes. It helps."

Once she left, I put my feet back down and typed *fukuoka* into the search bar. The map narrowed back to the southern portion of Japan. Would a person actually travel across a space as vast as half a country to simply see art? Or purchase a painting? Were BadDog's paintings even for sale? Or were they just there for the taking? And what constituted vastness? Was Japan even that big? Was the planet?

"You can always come to the library," I heard the clerk say from between two shelves, as if providing an answer to any of my questions, which she was not. I typed in *toronto* and started to print.

*

I returned to my apartment that day with many new maps in my pillowcase: Fukuoka to Tokyo. Toronto to Tokyo. Toronto to Fukuoka via Tokyo. The bus plus three trains, flight plus bus plus six subways, and feet plus ferry routes from Fukuoka to Taitō Ward. What light there was now came in through the window above the sink and split at the pipes, landing in two rectangles on the floor between the kitchenette and the bed. I placed the pillowcase in one and sat down in the other. Then the phone rang. I retrieved it from the bottom of the pillowcase.

"Are you okay?" said Sarah.

"Yes."

She inhaled like she was going to talk again, but then exhaled. But then she inhaled again and did talk.

"Because I just got this text from Hadir?"

"With Tacka Attack's photo?"

"Hadir texted me and said you showed up at his house last night on drugs. His words. But I was worried, because of yesterday."

"It was this morning, I've never used drugs, and Hadir spends too much time in a room with limited exposure to natural light."

"Are you okay, though? I mean, I know you're sad. It was really sad, what happened yesterday."

The more Sarah kept saying the words "sad" and "yesterday," the more I struggled to think of any other words I could use to respond to her question. So I said what I'd said the first time she asked: "Yes."

"Maybe I'll stop by," she said.

"On your way to where?"

The alarm went off on my phone. I held it out in front of myself and stared at the numbers: *10:59*.

"Hello?" I could hear Sarah calling from my hands. "Is that your phone?"

"Yes," I called back to her.

"Hello?"

Then the call ended. I turned off the alarm, connected to Ronda, found the first paper for the contest in the pillowcase and entered its website into the search bar. Where the *Click Here to Vote* box used to be, there was now a box that read, *Contest Closed. Results to be posted online after.*

I looked up at the wall beyond the bed, the only wall with something hung on it. Or stuck to it, I should say—a calendar, with a rolled-up bit of duct tape. Each previous month had also been duct-taped in order to hold up the page on the current one. For this month, the final of the year, there were only eleven days left that could potentially be what the web page had referred to as "after," and then the days would run out. So, in the event that "after" was not one of those eleven days, I would need a new calendar.

I called Sarah.

"Thank you," I said when she answered the phone.

"You're welcome. I just care about you."

"If you're stopping by anyway, could you please go to the hardware store and pick up a box of thumbtacks? You can add it to my tab. Also, another latte. You'll have to front the cash for that."

"Another?"

"Now is not the time to be cutting back on lattes," I said before dropping the phone back into the pillowcase. It also wasn't the time to be sitting around in a rectangle of light. I needed to get on all fours and find the pencil that I was pretty sure had rolled beneath the bed weeks, maybe months, ago.

*

Sarah soon arrived carrying a coffee tray, a box of thumbtacks and a plastic container of cookies, the only thing she ever baked and which always turned out tasting somewhat like kidney beans.

"You brought your cookies," I pointed out.

She smiled and set the container on the foot of the bed.

"Can I ask you a question that's semi-serious but non-judgemental?" she said.

"Yes."

"Are you in the midst of some sort of mental health crisis?"

"No, but why do you ask?"

"There are a bunch of papers spread out in a circle on your floor. And you're sitting in the middle of them. That's so much paper. Why are some of them wrinkled?"

"I fell in the snow."

"When?"

"This morning. I missed my stop, because of the darkness, or my thoughts, which were also, admittedly, dark, but not concerningly so, I don't think, and as a result I exited the streetcar via the stairs too fast at the next stop, and I, plus my pillowcase, fell in the snow."

"Your pillowcase?"

"The papers were inside of it."

Sarah looked up at the wall in front of me.

"Did you draw on the wall, Austin?"

"Yes."

"Is that a calendar?"

"It's a placeholder until I can get a real one," I said.

"Did you use a pencil?"

I tapped the pencil I'd tucked behind my ear. She squinted her eyes to try to see the calendar better.

"I think the easiest way to do this would be for one of us to be in charge of the papers, and one of us to be in charge of the thumbtacks," I said. "Since I know what order the papers were printed, why don't I hand them to you, and you can then pin them onto the wall."

"You're wearing the same clothes as yesterday," said Sarah. "Have you even taken off your shoes?"

"Not yet."

"What about sleep? Did you do that?"

I shrugged. She set the coffee tray on the counter, which took up the entire space of it, and picked out the box of thumbtacks from one of the cupholders. Then she came back to where I was, stepped over the papers so as to stand in front of the wall, and took the first page I handed to her from *Japan Views Lifestyle News in English*. She held it up beside the placeholder calendar.

"No," I said. "We need to start a new row."

*

Once all twenty-two sheets of paper had been transferred to the wall, Sarah and I stood side by side facing it, drinking a latte, if you were me, and sucking the tip of your tacking thumb, if you were Sarah. I directed her attention to the beginning of the plot.

"This is BadDog," I said. "He's a painter, sculptor, installation artist. You find his work around and in the street, if you look for it. The street being one that exists in Japan, presumably. He created a mural in Taitō Ward."

I pointed to Taitō Ward on the map of Tokyo.

"But what matters more is that he also created a painting of a three-and-a-half-pawed, no-eyed cat with orange fur, perched in a sphinx position on the edge of a table, which somehow ended up in the possession of Tacka Attack Love, a young woman living, in all likelihood, all the way over here."

I pointed to the map that illustrated the distance between Fukuoka and Tokyo. Then, to the map illustrating the distance between Toronto and Tokyo.

"Hadir, who lives 10,934 kilometres away from Tacka Attack Love, came across a photo of the painting on Instagram, and sent it to myself, Austin, who lives eleven kilometres away from Hadir, where, miraculously, I had just been holding a cat who was an exact replica of the cat in the photo of the painting, while he died. Or, the painting was a replica of the cat, when the cat was alive. You get what I mean."

"Did you ask Hadir how he came across the painting?" she asked.

"No."

"What about the girl on Instagram. Did you message her?"

"I can message her?"

"Show me this painting," she said.

I picked up the pillowcase from the floor and dumped out the phone onto the bed. Sarah picked it up and held it out to me.

"Just press the button," I said.

"There's no password?"

"Then go to the messages and look at the one from Hadir. The first one."

She tapped the screen.

"He called you a cracker," Sarah said.

"Scroll down."

She slid a finger over the screen. Her hands looked like a package of Mini Eggs with each of her nails painted a different pastel shade.

"How did you find time to both bake and make your nails look so beautiful?" I asked her.

She looked up at me and kind of smiled. Then she looked back down at the phone, and her expression changed to something else entirely. Her mouth even opened.

"Oh my god," she said.

"You see it, too?"

She lifted her mouth to the wall.

"Austin, what are the rest of these other papers for?"

"Well," I began. "This is the first page of a website where a vote collection for an art contest had been taking place for an unspecified period of time prior to today. These are the biographies of the artists who had been chosen as the contest's finalists, and this is the last page of the website, with the information about where Hōnto No Kimochi Gallery and Café is located."

"What does that have to do with this?" she said, turning the phone toward the wall, as if the wall would answer her.

"BadDog entered the contest. Voting has closed as of 10:59 Eastern Standard Time this morning, and the winner will be announced online after."

"After what?"

I shrugged.

"Hence the calendars," I said.

Sarah dropped her hand with the phone in it to her side, then walked like she was sleepwalking back to the bed where she sat down and opened the container of her bean-like cookies.

"I know I made these for you, but I'm going to need to eat one," she said.

"You can eat them all, if that's what you need."

Her eyes were weird as she bit one in half. Not blinking, but also like they were not seeing anything, either. Because a lot of crumbs tumbled down the front of her sweater and onto the bed and the floor, and she just kept moving her jaw up and down like they hadn't, like her mouth was a puppet's mouth being controlled by a ghost hand.

"So, is this all a big coincidence?" she eventually said.

"Do you think that's a possibility?"

"The artist could have had a cat just like the one you had. Or, if Scoot did belong to this artist, he coincidentally found his way to you."

"How?"

"I guess by boat, or something."

"And Hadir found Scoot. In painting form. Less than one hour after our visit to the vet."

She finished the cookie, then looked down at her sweater and knocked the crumbs off it. The ones that had ended up on her cheeks and lips she wiped away with the back of her hand. "And the reward?"

"For his return. Or information pertaining to it, I assume."

"Which you have."

I nodded.

"How much do you think—actually, no." She waved her hand. "Don't answer that."

I shrugged.

"It would seem Scoot is very important to him. Was. Enough for this artist to have painted his portrait."

"Let's message the girl," she said.

I looked at the time. "It's after midnight in Fukuoka."

She held the phone to me. "Everyone does things whenever they want. Because everyone keeps their phone on silent."

I took the phone. "What should I say? Never mind, I know what to say."

"What are you going to say?"

I opened Instagram to search for Tacka. But the moment I did, I was immediately confronted by a new photo, posted, as it could only have been, by @tacka_attack_love, mere minutes ago. I turned the screen to Sarah.

"Does she know that we're talking about her right now?"

Sarah didn't answer. Instead, her eyes started to go weird again and she reached for another cookie.

"What is it now?" I said, placing my hand on her shoulder as she bit into the cookie.

"At." Her jaw moved.

"At? That? That picture?"

She continued to eat her cookie. I moved directly in front of her, and even squatted a little, trying to make her eyes focus on mine.

"Sarah," I said. "What about that picture?"

Some crumbs fell from her mouth and onto my shoes as she whispered, "Another coincidence."

*

At her behest, we took our conversation out for a walk. Sarah explained to me that she needed some air, and that also the photo posted by Tacka Attack Love was of an orchid identical to Aisopos's, which also felt a lot like hers, because she cared for it so consistently.

"It has a personality," she said.

"I'm sure lots of people feel that way about their orchids. Including Tacka Attack Love. Which would explain why she would take a photograph of her own."

"And then post it on Instagram at the exact moment that I, an orchid-minder of an all-white orchid with skinny petals that fan out like a firework identical to the one in the photo, am with you, the person with the original coincidental connection to a photo posted to her account, in your apartment, while you're in the process of thinking up a message to send to her?"

She was right. There was no point in trying to normalize the situation; the orchid was a part of this, too. But—was it connected to BadDog? Was there, for some reason, an ominous message being relayed to Sarah regarding this elegant species of plantae via my phone? I hoped not. I hoped really hard not. We reached the crosslane in the laneway, and Sarah pointed left.

"How about this?" I said. "Dear Miss Love, what is your relation to the subject of the painting in the photograph that is currently posted in the fifth—actually, now the sixth position on your Instagram account, and also, what prompted you to share your most recent photograph of an orchid at the moment that you did?"

"That's good. But perhaps you should explain who you are first, so she doesn't feel stalked. People tend to feel stalked when they receive a message from another person who hasn't provided any traceable evidence regarding their own identity, especially when that person is asking a very specific question about the other person's Instagram account."

That made sense.

"But who am I?" I asked Sarah.

The cross-lane ended and we came to the street in front of the park.

"This way," she answered. We crossed over to the park path. "Your name is Austin. You live in Toronto, Canada, and you possess three quarters of a Media Arts and Animation certificate. People also tend to be less fearful of educated people."

"But we're telling her I'm only three quarters of the way educated. That leaves a whole quarter of my personality for her to be afraid of."

"Fill that quarter with only good qualities."

Only good qualities? I was neither fully educated nor as naturally smart as Sarah. It would probably be easier to come up with a list of my not-so-good qualities and let Tacka Attack Love deduce the rest of my personality from there.

"Do you know how Aisopos came into possession of this orchid?" I asked Sarah.

"Walmart," she said.

"Thee Walmart?"

"Thee means you."

"The one you worked at? Where we purchased the cougar food, and the litter and litter tray, and treats?"

"That's the closest one."

I looked down at the ground, at the garbage spilled all over the snow from a bin that had been tipped sideways and was now blocking the pathway in front of us. It was true that people did usually just go to their nearest Walmart whenever they needed to go to Walmart. But what was it about this Walmart specifically that seemed to be pulling everything into its orbit? Or, ejecting it outward?

"We have to turn back now," I said.

"Yeah. Ew," Sarah agreed.

*

Huffing hot air between my hands, I warmed the key to unlock the padlock, then lifted the bolt of the steel door. Sarah looked at the clock-face pendant on her necklace.

"I have a job interview in one hour," she said.

"What's the job?"

"Temporary typist at a talent agency."

"An office job?" I said.

"It pays one dollar more per hour than minimum wage. I'll call you later. Eat the cookies before I come back."

"Yes. I will."

I knew as I went inside the building and back up the elevator to my apartment without Sarah that afternoon that I wasn't going to eat the cookies but instead hide them in an empty egg carton that I kept in the refrigerator for the purpose of hiding Sarah's cookies in until I got around to taking the garbage out. So, as I finally took off my shoes, as well as my socks, because both were wet from walking through the snow, and sat on the bed facing the wall of papers with my red, sort of hurting toes tucked inside the pillowcase, I began my list with the word *perjurer*. Then I reached over to the nightstand and opened the drawer where Scoot's treats, purchased from the Walmart in question, were still not hidden, because he'd figured out that that was where they were as soon as I put them in there, and so, consequently, had immediately taken to sitting on top of the nightstand and reaching over the edge with his full front paw to try and open the drawer himself, resulting in my having to place the lamp, which he couldn't see but that was normally set there, onto the floor, so he wouldn't knock it off. I examined the package of treats. They were best before 21/12/19. Exactly two years from the date of the day it, at that moment, was. They also suggested I should shake them, as indicated within a purple star on the front bottom left corner, and that they had been manufactured in the USA. I closed the drawer and picked up my phone.

 The manufacturing headquarters of Scoot's cat treats was located in St. Louis, Missouri, even though they were apparently Canada's most trusted brand of cat treats. I searched: *do orchids also grow in st louis missouri* and tapped the first thing to appear below the search bar, which was a link to a page of the website for the Missouri Botanical Garden. Below the heading of the page that read *Orchids: About the Collection* was an image of an all-white orchid with skinny petals that fanned out like a firework, identical to Tacka Attack Love's, and thus, Aisopos's, and below that image was the word *Neofinetia*, which I pencilled onto the nightstand with the pencil I'd tucked behind my ear, then re-tucked, before typing the term into a new search bar. Neofinetia, also known as the Samurai Orchid, were a species of orchid native to Japan. They lived year-round but only flowered once per year for approximately two weeks, during which time they were extremely fragrant. I closed the page. Somehow, like Canada acquiring a package of cat treats from Missouri, Missouri had acquired a species of orchids from Japan. As had Aisopos, and by proxy, Sarah, the person proximal to myself, and therefore, also near-at-hand to the preliminary subject abreast of myself, Scoot.

It was here that I paused to imagine Scoot pausing to clean the nook behind his ear with his functional paw for five minutes, or maybe longer. I used to think he did that to place me in a trance. Because there wasn't much there, only about a millimetre of fuzz that had grown in after a week had passed without lice eating away at it anymore. Now, though, I think it was that he was proud of that growth and was happy to once again have something in that spot to clean. He wanted to take his time. He wanted to nurture it. Who knows how long the spot had been bald for?

Someone. Someone knew. And that someone may or may not be searching for Scoot, myself or a large portion of reward. I snapped out of Scoot's memory trance to look for a piece of paper, but all the paper in the apartment was tacked to the wall. The only pressed and dyed pulp at my disposal was a napkin, folded and set neatly upon the coffee tray alongside the full latte Sarah had apparently been too weirded out to drink any of. I stood from the bed, shuffled my pillowcase-encased feet over to the countertop and tore a small square from the napkin to cover the hole of the lid to save it for her for later. The rest I spread open on the floor, then squatted down and took the pencil back out from behind my ear.

First, I wrote the word *Neofinetia* and circled it. From there, three branches grew: *Aisopos, Missouri, Tacka Attack Love*. From

Aisopos: *Walmart*. From Walmart: *cat treats*. Cat treats connected to Missouri. From *Tacka Attack Love*, there was both a connection to *Hadir*, and *photo of painting of cat*, which I also circled. This connected to *BadDog*, circled. Circled three times to make it bolder. From *BadDog*, I drew branches to the words *contest* and *mural*, and lastly, from the word *mural*, a branch to the word *animalism*.

I stood and looked down at the map. Then I picked it up from the floor. Carried it, plus a thumbtack, over to the wall. I stuck the thumbtack between my front teeth and held up the napkin with both hands, moving it in front of the papers to find a spot for it that wouldn't obscure any other information. Which was tricky, because the lines of light from the window had moved upward and were now directly behind my shoulders, beaming to the point where my arms were elevated, making the napkin semi-see-through, which meant that I sort of had to guess. And which also meant that, while in doing such guesswork, I would coincidentally discover the thing I would discover next.

The phone rang. I spat out the thumbtack then tried to sprint toward the bed, which resulted in my falling to the floor. From the floor, I reached over the edge of the mattress to answer it.

"Sarah?" I shouted.

"What's wrong? Is Sarah missing?"

It was Dan.

"The map I just drew is the same shape as the country of Japan," I shouted again.

Dan didn't shout back.

"Is Sarah okay?" he said.

"I don't know. She's at a job interview now, but she hasn't had any caffeine."

"I just wanted to check in after yesterday," he said.

There was that word again. Yesterday.

"When I hold up the napkin, the light permeates the thin material and makes it semi-see-through," I told him.

"Can you repeat what you just said?"

"When I hold up the napkin, upon which I drew a map of clues, the light from the window permeates the thin material, and the material thus becomes semi-see-through. So, when I hold the clue map over the map of Japan, I can see through it to the other side. As a result, I can see that they are, in fact, the same shape. The maps."

"When did you last see Sarah?"

"When our walk ended, before she left for her job interview. People are disrespectful. Just because this is a city and not a forest doesn't mean it's okay to leave garbage everywhere. There's still an environment, even if it's not so obvious."

"Is this drawing stuff for work, Austin? Like, did you get some work?"

"It's work, but not the kind you're referring to."

"So, it's not work."

Sarah told me that Dan could be a judgemental asshole sometimes.

"Buddy?" he said.

"Okay, Dan, I appreciate you checking in on me."

"Karly wants to know if you can come over for dinner. But I don't know if that's such a good idea right now. Because the baby."

"The baby's not born yet."

"It doesn't need to be born."

"To what?"

"Get affected."

"What is she making for dinner?"

"It's your mental state, Austin."

What the hell was he talking about? "My mental state is no different than it was the last time I saw Karly, and she was fertilized then," I said.

"It's just the stress. We don't want to stress the baby."

"I'm not really clear on whether or not I'm being invited to dinner."

Dan sighed. "You can come, but like, you really have to try. For Karly."

While I also wasn't clear on what Dan was asking me to try, I had enough on my wall to deal with already, and I knew that staying on the phone with him any longer was only going to lead to more judgment. "I love Karly. She's like an axolotl," I said.

"What? Just come around four tomorrow. Don't bring anything. Like, I don't know what you're making, but don't bring it to show us."

"I couldn't even if I wanted to."

"K. Bye for now."

"Wait," I said before he hung up.

It was silent.

"Are you still there?" I said.

"Yes, but I don't know why. What is it?"

I climbed forward onto the edge of the bed and sat, again, facing the wall. Except I didn't sit so much as I kind of gave out.

"I'm like a newt," I told Dan.

"K. I'm going to tell Karly what you just told me, and then I'm going to text you to confirm whether or not dinner's still on. Maybe, while you're waiting, you could get some rest?"

When Dan hung up, I noticed that it was more quiet than it was in the night, even. And the light beam was gone, and very soon it would just be dark again. Black dark. But that didn't change the fact that it was the middle of day, which would imply that whatever it was I was doing, in Dan's opinion, I could just put it down and take a rest from it.

    I kicked off the pillowcase and went over to the counter. Drinking Sarah's latte that I was supposed to be saving for her was an action I took—not a quality, but it was still bad. I was a liar and generally untrustworthy. I was partially educated in Media Arts and Animation, had played the guitar since I was five years old and enjoyed folding laundry, although, for some reason, there hadn't been any to fold lately. And the reason for my sending this message on this day that is night in Japan is to ask how it was that you came into possession of the painting featured in the sixth position on your Instagram account, by the artist known as BadDog, from Taitō Ward, Tokyo.

    That was what I sent to Tacka Attack Love three weeks and one full day post-adoption of my now-dead pet, Scoot.

*

I followed the footprints of my and Sarah's shoes down the laneway to the cross-lane, across the street and back through the park along the pathway to the garbage blockade, where I pulled the tipped bin upright. I picked up a piece of trash that was technically a recyclable and dropped it into the bin. Then I picked up what might have been a mango. And then a newspaper, with thick brown liquid dripping from it, which I let go of, and dropped back to the ground. I couldn't clean up anymore. It was just too gross. That's what I told the woman in the red wool poncho anyway, who was watching me from five feet down the path.

"People are animals," she said, before cutting off through the snow to continue on her way.

Animals.

Red.

Poncho.

Poncho is like a kaftan.

Wearing a kaftan in public.

I took a sprinting jump over the garbage and kept sprinting once I'd landed.

CHAPTER 4

Chamomile Tea and Half a Million Dollars

The yellow sunbeams to the right of the giant white block letters buzzing above the half-empty parking spot, within which I stood next to a Jeep that was way over the line, made everything seem more dark somehow. All around, people pushing carts sounded like a bunch of prisoners dragging their chains. My hands were cold. It was a really shitty evening. But I had to go to Walmart.

Inside, the store was too bright and all of the shoppers looked anemic. The whole place was like a messy closet, unfolded and de-hangered clothes abandoned everywhere as I passed each aisle on my way to the pet section. Mittens stuck on the necks of mouthwash bottles. Snow boots in the middle of places where I was about to step, tripping me. It was chaos. Until I reached the final section. There, everything ended. Three separate women even turned 180 degrees right behind me as if it didn't even exist. As if I, standing just past the edge of the patio furniture, was a ghost.

It was a nerve-wracking experience, walking on the sides of my shoes so the soles wouldn't squeak, to the place where Scoot's old cat food was, knowing that no one might come if I screamed. I reminded myself that I had reasonably long arms, though; that if it came to it, I could push a lot of product off a shelf at once to create a temporary barricade, giving myself enough of a head start out of there. So that was the plan. If it came to it. I shifted onto the balls of my feet, ready to sprint.

The kaftan man was sitting on the dog food stack again, though he was no longer wearing his dress, but an oversized hockey jersey and a pair of basketball shorts. He dipped a tea bag into a mug with a $3.99 price sticker stuck to its side.

"You," I called to him.

He turned his face to mine, but kept his eyes closed.

"Where did you get boiled water from?" I said. "And since when are you into sports?"

He tilted his head as though he were feeling coy. I tried to get a look around the area without losing track of him. Next to the dog food was a three-tier cat tree with a box for an electric kettle tucked at its base. He reached through the cut-out window of one of the tree's caves and extracted a package of chamomile, opening his eyes only then, as he held it out for me like some kind of stolen, drugged offering.

"I don't want tea," I said. "I want answers."

"You looked cold," he said, with what sounded like a put-on British accent.

"Excuse me?" I said. "Can you repeat that?"

"You looked cold."

It was definitely a put-on British accent.

"You didn't see me until after you got the tea."

He shrugged.

"I have some questions for you," I said. "And you're going to answer them, to the best of your ability. Otherwise I'm telling the manager-on-duty what's really going on here."

"Yvette? Yvette's on break in twenty. She's coming for tea."

"You live here," I said.

"Mm mm," he said, shaking his head no.

"Mm hm," I said, shaking mine yes. "And you had my friend Sarah fired, too. Over fish food. Seriously. Do you have any idea what it's like to have to job hunt in this city?"

He uncrossed then recrossed his legs the other way.

"I don't recall there being a Sarah who worked here."

"There's probably five Sarahs working here right now. It's one of the most common names in North America."

"Well, I don't recall."

"What do you guys do? Just like, set up camp and create murals wherever you please?"

"Oh," he said, sort of tensing his whole body, squeezing his thighs together, and interlocking his fingers around his mug. Then with a shudder, released. I was ready to sprint. "I don't know what you mean by creating murals," he said. "But it sounds quite lovely."

"Tell me about your connection to BadDog."

"I don't listen to rap music."

"What music do you listen to?"

"Lately, Christmas songs." He stuck his pinky up from his mug and pointed it toward the display of outdoor furniture six metres away. "But I have to go over there."

"Ah hah," I shouted. "You admit it."

"I don't recall the accusation."

"Just answer me this: are you working alone? Or are you part of an organization of some kind, with some leader some place, coordinating the movement of orchids and feral cats?"

He rotated his hips until the toes of his topmost foot were pointed directly at me, then he smiled and, somehow, dilated his own pupils.

"For how would you define this word, *feral*?"

*

Sprinting past the checkouts and through the automatic doors, I wondered why it was that security duty at the Walmart closest to Aisopos and Sarah's house had been delegated to a ninety-year-old man with a back like a turtle's shell, who could never stop a thief, let alone a full-tilt animalist from stealing an electric kettle. I sort of slid across the icy parking lot until I ducked into the bus shelter at the bottom of it, where I took out my phone.

Why did you tell Dan about the thing with school?

I waited for Hadir to answer while a woman carrying a boxed microwave walked directly into me, then continued trying to push through my body to get to the bench behind it. I stepped out of the bus shelter.

That you quit?
Why would you tell him anything about me at all?
Just shooting the shit and it came up natural.
Why are you shooting shit with Dan?
Shit son whats the bfd?
How do you know her?
Wat?
Tacka.

??

Attack Love.

As the bus approached, the microwave stood to push me in front of it. I ended up in the ditch, where the slush was up to my ankles.

Ohhhh, Hadir replied.

"Hurry up," the driver shouted. I looked up from my phone. He seemed really pissed off.

"I don't have money," I said.

"Come on, man," he said, pulling the lever to close the door like he wanted to snap it off and chuck it at my face. I went back into the shelter.

?? I messaged Hadir.

DOTA.

She's a player?

Ya but not exactly.

After that, he sent me a dancing cartoon character that was supposed to look like himself, implying that he was not going to be forthcoming with any of the information that I was looking for. Either because he felt like annoying me, as was commonly the case, or because something else was going on inside the internet that he might even be a part of. Could BadDog have any relation to an online fantastical dystopian universe? Could a cat? I put my phone in my pocket and looked back again to the artificial sun above the store entrance, farther away now but still close enough to illuminate the tops of my hands and therefore, I could assume, my face. Like it was telling me it could see me. That it was watching me. That I'd better tread lightly through the slush. But was I treading? I might have been. I thought of Anna in her car, hopeless under the eye of whatever the equivalent to a Walmart marquee was in

England. How Grear had said "car park" instead of "parking lot." I couldn't trust my oldest friend. I asked the person now inside the bus shelter next to me, holding a snow shovel and a box of diapers, what he was thinking about.

"My wife?" he responded.

*

As I turned down the laneway behind my building, Sarah emerged from the other end. We walked toward each other and met at the door.

"Everything moves in a zigzag pattern," I said to her.

"I know what you mean," she said.

"How did your interview go?"

"Hard to say."

"Always is."

I turned the key in the padlock and she lifted the bolt. I followed her inside, then cranked down the elevator.

"What's the story with Yvette?" I said.

"Manager Yvette?"

"The only Yvette I know. Do you know more?"

"Yes."

"So, yes, then. Manager Yvette."

"She's a sad person and I hate her. That was a bad thing to say. I don't hate people. But if I came close to it with one person, it would be her."

"She knows about the guy in the pet section."

"The squatter?"

"He's more than a squatter. He may even be framing me for murder to claim the much reward for himself."

I gestured for Sarah to go into the elevator first. As I cranked us upward, she fixed her eyes ahead and squinted as though there were something in the distance and not a closed metal gate three inches from her face. Once we were back in the apartment, she went straight to the counter where the empty tray that should have held her latte sat crooked. She straightened it.

"I'm really sorry," I said.

She didn't make a sound while lifting herself onto the barber stool. I could tell she felt like she'd deserved to have her latte stolen after what she'd said about Yvette. I went over and put my hand on her shoulder.

"Can I offer you tap water?"

She moved her head in a circle, the meaning of which I couldn't determine. I went to the sink anyway and filled the small white mug that had come with the apartment with warm water. When I gave it to her, she wrapped her hands around it, lacing her index fingers through the handle.

"When it comes to duties, what are Yvette's?" I asked her.

Sarah took a sip from the mug, I think to keep herself from scoffing.

"She spends most of her time up in that dingy office that overlooks the store playing Donut County on her phone and eating Party Mix. She tells the same two cashiers, Jenna and Eliana, that they're short one dollar and twenty-five cents every time she counts their tills, and relieves them four minutes late for their break, every break, every shift. She might come down from her lair once in a while and pretend to put away clothes left at the fitting rooms, but in all actuality, she's just shopping for herself."

"How does she keep her job?"

"Regional manager's daughter."

"Nepotism."

"She leaves cheese stains on the clothes. This is so bad, awful."

I sat down on the floor in front of her even though it was wet from the snow of my shoes. Drops of snow water dripped from the bottoms of Sarah's boots, too, which she normally would have removed at the door, but were, at this moment, propped on the footrest of the stool.

"It sounds to me like you're merely stating facts," I said. "You don't have to worry about being perfect around me."

She made a head circle again. I placed a hand on the toe of her boot.

"She once told Eliana to hurry up in the washroom over the P.A."

I nodded okay, as a way to tell her that I didn't need her to talk about Yvette anymore—it was obvious what kind of person she was. Corrupt, and stupid. Sarah rested the mug on one of her knees, then one of her cheeks in one of her hands. Why had I drank her latte? It wouldn't have been hot at this point, but it might have at least affected an association with being comforted. I stood from the floor and went over to the place where I'd tucked the napkin map to keep it from drifting away in a flutter from a breeze created by the movement of my body in the room: under the sheet at the head of the bed.

"I know that was hard to do," I said, as I peeled back the sheet. "But, look. See?"

Sarah came over to the bed.

"Oh my god," she said, after studying the napkin for a moment.

"Yeah," I said.

"It's the shape of Japan," she yelled.

I picked it up and held it against the wall, then took the pencil from behind my ear. Extending south-left of the leftmost branch, I drew a new branch from *Walmart* that led to the word: *corruption*. I held it over the real map of Japan.

"It's the final bit of tiny islands down there at the bottom."

The phone rang. I took it out of my pocket and threw it on the bed. But it continued anyway.

"Who is it?" she said.

"I don't know yet."

It kept ringing. Until it stopped. Then we both went over to the bed and I reached down to poke the button, after which I immediately retracted my arm and turned my face away. Sarah peered over the edge of the bed and, with no mug of water to prevent her from doing so, scoffed.

"Hadir," she said.

I picked up the phone and tapped his name to immediately call him back.

"Why are you calling me?" I said when he answered.

"Dan wasn't picking up."

I gave the phone to Sarah and turned to face the other way.

"He refuses to look at you," she said into the phone. "Don't be a retard."

I looked over my shoulder at her.

"Says Hadir," she clarified. "No, he's only looking at me. He thought that was from me."

I took the phone back from Sarah.

"Explain," I said to Hadir, as she huddled closer to hear.

"Why are you so obsessed?" he said.

"I'm not."

"I already told you. *DOTA*."

"But she's not a player?"

"She doesn't play. She joins for the chats."

"She speaks English?" said Sarah.

"Not really. But that's kind of the point."

Hadir was really getting on my nerves.

"Be less ambiguous," I said.

"Please," Sarah added.

"ASMR. She meets me in the game, then voice chats with me to do it."

"What is ASMR?" I asked Sarah.

"Like automatic something something whatever," said Hadir.

"I'm asking Sarah."

"It feels good," he said. "Tingly. Like, everywhere. Feel me?"

Sarah took a step away from us both.

"You're making Sarah feel uncomfortable," I told Hadir.

"What? It's natural."

"Are you in a kind of relationship?"

Hadir laughed once, loud and wetly.

"No, bro. Girl gets her pay."

I hung up the phone, then sent a message to Hadir saying I never wanted to talk to him again.

"I'd like to go get a latte now," said Sarah.

*

Twenty minutes later, she sat beside me on the carpeted floor of the library, legs outstretched so they were both beneath my chair, an atlas the size of an entire coffee table covered in maroon fabric with black stains opened upon her lap. She sipped her latte over Peru.

"What are those black stains?" I said.

"Ink or mould, or both. I'm trying not to touch it."

"ASMR can be caused by gum chewing," I told her.

"Now I can never chew gum again."

It could also be caused by keyboard taps, crinkling cellophane, page turning, pen scratching, whispering and hair brushing, but I kept all of that to myself. After printing this information from Wikipedia, as well as the information page of the orchid collection at the Missouri Botanical Gardens, I searched: *asmr dota*, and a long list of YouTube channels appeared. I played the first video on the list and a whispering British man who sounded like he couldn't stop licking his teeth led me through the process of selecting some sort of monster to watch run around Mordor.

"I can't understand anything they're saying," I said, clicking ahead in the stream. "Something about collecting something?"

Sarah looked up from the book.

"I think you're supposed to wear headphones."

"I don't own headphones."

She unzipped her jacket and pulled out a pair of earbuds tied together like a bow. I plugged them into the computer and started the video over again.

"I still can't make anything out," I said. "This doesn't feel good at all. It's just frustrating."

"Maybe they aren't doing it right."

I stopped the video and searched: *good asmr*. In the first video, a young woman with a lot of freckles holding a steaming mug whispered, "Hey guys."

"I just got my nails done," she continued, drumming the golden tips steadily against the ceramic. They glittered beneath a string of white Christmas lights hung above her head. "Hope ya'll like them."

It suddenly felt like ants were crawling up my neck. The video had over 800,000 views.

"Whatever this is, it seems like a lot of people are into it," I said. "Who knows how many are out there running private sessions like Tacka."

"I wonder how much she makes," said Sarah.

I paused the video and searched: *how much money can you make doing asmr?* The first answer I received suggested half a million dollars per year, if you were good at it.

"Would knowing the answer to that ruin money for you?"

Sarah sighed like it most likely would and turned the twenty-two-inch yellowing page to Bolivia with her own enchanting and semi-sparkling fingernails. Sarah definitely had the same fairy-like quality as the freckled YouTuber. With practice, she could probably make a lot of people very happy. I unpaused the video and watched as the young woman held the tag of a tea bag between her thumb and fingertip, lifting the bag out and letting it gently kerplunk back in, over and over again. I couldn't tell whether the crawling ants felt good or not. They definitely tingled. I stopped the video, closed the browser and slid from the chair to join Sarah on the floor, stretching my legs beside hers to prop up the half of the book that didn't fit upon her own lap.

"Thanks," she said. "It's a really big world."

"Is it, though?"

"The surface area of the Earth alone is over five hundred million square kilometres. The distance from where we are sitting right now to your apartment is barely even one of those."

I ran a fingertip over the deckled edge of the pages. Sarah did the same on her side. It was as soft as a patch of new cat fur growing in. I scratched at some of the black stuff on the corner of the inside cover. It flaked off and got stuck beneath my nail. Then I started on a new bit of it.

"What was the last normal thing we did together?" I asked Sarah.

"We had lobster mac and cheese from the deli at the grocery store and watched forty-five minutes of *The Silence of the Lambs* on your phone. Then the internet stopped working, and we took turns playing your guitar."

I looked above Sarah's head and tried to visualize the calendar on the wall in my apartment.

"Four days ago," I said.

"Yes."

"It feels as though time has passed vastly."

"I know."

"Yet, we could have travelled from Toronto to Tokyo and back three times. And then once more to Tokyo."

"Go figure."

"Do you think Hadir knows more than he's letting on?"

If she wore glasses, Sarah would have taken them off her face at that moment, folded their arms neatly together and placed them on the bench in front of her before clasping her hands and glaring down her nose at me. "Hadir could know everything there is to know and still not realize he knows anything at all." That seemed like an accurate judgment. She slid her legs out from beneath the atlas. "Help me," she said.

I lifted the top side of the cover while Sarah lifted the bottom, and together we closed the world in on itself. Then we lifted the book and put it back onto the display shelf above a placard that read *Do Not Remove*. Sarah brushed her hands together, as if to dust them off, and grabbed the pillowcase from the back of the chair where I'd been sitting.

"You have some printing to pick up," she said.

I did. But I was starting to wonder if, at that point, I wasn't actually just burying the answer deeper within the wall.

"Maybe it's that you're building your puzzle in a zigzag pattern," said Sarah. "As opposed to starting with all of the flat-edged pieces until the frame has been built, and then flipping the other ones right side up so you can sort them out by colour."

Maybe. Maybe not. But certainly, it would be tricky to conceptualize such a concept with many rectangular sheets of white paper.

*

I walked Sarah back to Aisopos's house after that, after what felt like the end to a very long day that she'd never asked to have, and even still, in the skinny path formed by the packed-down snow of her steps from that morning, she took the time to rub both my bare hands between her mittened ones to try and warm them up.

"Don't," I said. "I can't even feel them."

"That's the problem."

She continued for another minute or so. Behind her, a light turned on in the living room window.

"Did we wake him up?" I whispered.

She looked over her shoulder. "What time is it?"

"I'd check my phone but you have my hands."

She leaned forward and pulled back the sleeve of her coat with her teeth.

"Look at my watch," she said.

I did. It was too dark to see, though.

"Back up a few steps with me."

We shuffled together approximately five steps backwards until we were under the light of the streetlamp. I looked at her watch again.

"Five after nine."

"Hm. He is usually in bed by nine. Then doesn't wake up until one, when he has a sandwich, and then goes back to bed until five, when wakes up again, has a sandwich, then goes back to bed until six."

The window went dark. We shuffled forward. Sarah slowly let go of my hands while rolling my fingers into fists, then tugged down my sleeves to cover them up.

"Acid reflux, perhaps," she said. "Put those in your pockets now."

I did.

"Keep them there until you get home. Okay, I'm going to go inside now."

"Okay."

But she didn't. Not right away, anyway. It seemed like she was waiting for something, though I didn't ask what for. Just waited for her to finish waiting. When whatever happened finally did, she turned around and followed her path to the door, and once she was inside, I could hear her boots clunk lightly against the floor, and then the lock turn on the knob after she closed the second door. Again, a light turned on in the window, only this time, it wasn't as bright. More eleven-inch-laptop-screen-white. I wondered what Sarah might make herself to eat then, after preparing Aisopos's sandwiches, and what she'd watch on her computer while she ate it. I'm sure if I just went up and knocked on the door she'd invite me inside to have some and watch it with her. But I wasn't going to do that. Because someone else was walking up the street at a really quick pace then, and while I couldn't make them out very well, it appeared they were walking on stilts and wearing an overcoat with sleeves fabricated to look like bird wings.

So instead, I started to sprint, first down Sarah's footpath until I cut out to form my own, then through the backyard, and over to the adjacent street, where I continued to sprint down one tire path in the road until reaching the main road, where the sidewalk was clear, and even still I sprinted from there, six streets east, until I reached the laneway behind the factory and found my own footprints from earlier that day, iced over like they were fossilized now. I sprinted in those, next to Sarah's fossilizations, which looked like they were sprinting along with me because of the speed at which my eyes were moving, until I was at the door, where I took my fists out of my pockets to turn them back into hands, between the palms of which I pressed my key, so hard it was like I was trying to turn it into a dove. And then, maybe, the dove would fly up to the top of the building where it would find a nook to nest in, and by spring, there'd be more doves, and their gentle cooing would produce better tingles than any teeth-licking half-millionaire on YouTube ever could, if passersby should choose to pause and actually listen to them.

Just as I was about to release my dove, I felt my phone vibrate in my coat.

It's fine.

What?

What is? I typed with my thumb, still squeezing the key with the other four fingers.

Dinner. You can come.

I wanted to tell Dan that I had never asked to come over for dinner in the first place. But my thumb was already losing the blood Sarah had coaxed back into it, and I still needed to open the door. So all I said was, *K.*

Tomorrow at four.

He was just assuming I would have no other plans by almost 21:30 the night before tomorrow?

K, I said again, then put my phone back in my pocket and stuck my thumb in my mouth. But then pulled it out and took out my phone again. At the top right corner of the new icon on my home screen was a small red number one, much the same as that which had appeared in my virtual shopping cart when I'd hypothetically considered purchasing a black canvas tote bag with white print almost twenty-four hours previous to this moment.

Austin.

Three small dots pulsated below the message. I figured that meant more was coming. I breathed in and out fast, forgetting all about my now wet thumb, until the dots disappeared, at which point I forgot about my breath, too. A message appeared across the chat telling me that my internet connection had been lost. I looked up at the door, and then above the frame of it, up the wall of the building and all the way to the steam bubbling over from the roof. I knew I couldn't see Ronda—there were no windows on the back side of the building. Why was I wasting time trying? With one hand, I turned the key in the padlock, lifted the bolt, pulled open the door, cranked myself up the elevator shaft, then emerged through the gate, waving the phone around the narrow hallway space in front of my apartment until I'd re-established a connection. A message had appeared.

Cat no. But something I had lost, too.

She did know English. I started to type a response. Then Dan appeared.

We're inviting you into our home, buddy.

I didn't understand. He knew how phones worked. I couldn't just message him back without first exiting the chat I was currently having with a person in Japan.

You are like a person who snorkels, I told him. Then switched back to Tacka. *What have you*, I began to type, until Dan cut in, again.

Just remember, I'm your family, bud. Without me you pretty much have literally nothing.

Dan needed to wait a second. I went back to Tacka to finish my message, and saw I'd already accidentally sent the first three quarters of it, to which she'd already responded with a number, 20. Twenty? Twenty what? Dollars?

lost? I finished.

You were? she said.

Dollars? Years?

23, I said.

Then a moment passed where no one said anything. The screen went dark, and I was standing in a hallway with no lights on in it, listening to the tick-tocking of the pipes hidden in the walls around me, unable to see my own hand. Until the screen lit back up.

Same to her.

I turned the phone, still lit with Tacka's message, outward, so I could find the knob to my door. Once inside, I turned on the light.

I'd have three other brothers to get through first.

CHAPTER 5

An Axolotl

Before nothingness.

I switched back to Tacka.

Her?

Waiting for a response, I looked once again at the photo in which she was wearing her turtle-shell headphones. The background was dark, save for a tiny glowing sphere, approximately one-third of which existed outside the left frame of the photo, like a little waxing gibbous moon above and beyond her pointy shoulder. Whatever light source was lighting her head was positioned in front of her, where the photo was also being taken from. So, probably a computer doing both things simultaneously. Which also meant that it was possible that this specific photo could have been taken prior to, or post, a private ASMR session in a DOTA chat, perhaps, even, the definitive session with Hadir that would have prompted his further looking up of Tacka Attack Love on Instagram, discovery of the photo of the painting of Scoot, and sending of the photo to me, Austin. So actually, post-session most likely. Again, it had been liked by @maki18892 and @rockparty. I tapped @rockparty.

Rock Party had short, choppy blond hair, but in another picture it was more orange. In another one, it was bright red and styled into a mohawk. They wore collared shirts with the collar turned up, and a yellow, rubbery-looking overcoat, opened to display a golden waistband through which some kind of fancy stick was stuck. They also wore black eyeliner, silver eyeshadow, red contact lenses and black gloves covering exceptionally long-seeming fingers, which were either fanned along their stick or resting up near their pale beige lips. They were both pretty and handsome, fascinating and intimidating. They were like a hero.

It was hard to get my eyes to look away from them and over to any other details within the photos. When I managed to do so, however, I discovered Rock Party took their photos in the same spot nearly every time, in what appeared to be some sort of dressing room, with a green curtain covering the wall behind them, and the corner of a whitish-brownish table protruding five millimetres into frame. In fact, I counted thirty-two photos of Rock Party in this place before finding them in a different place—a garden of some sort, where they were seated on a rounded rock in front of a pond sipping a drink through a straw. They weren't wearing their gloves or yellow overcoat, either, only an oversized black sweater over top black jogging pants, and a pair of very clean white, red and yellow running shoes. I zoomed in on a huddle of flowers betwixt the greenery surrounding the pond; there was no doubting what my eyes were seeing there—Neofinetia.

Tacka responded.

Sorry so have travel store. Her same 23. 20.

Who was she talking about?

You Tokyo? she continued.

I Toronto, I said. *You Tokyo? To purchase the painting from BadDog?*

The three dots appeared. I waited. After some time, all Tacka finally said was, *No.*

Then how did you get the painting? I replied.

Again, dots.

Her Tokyo.

Okay.

Did Her mail it to you?

She responded right away this time, but again, with only the word, *No.* I waited to see if more dots would appear. Did Tacka think that no meant yes? Or was she simply saying no as a way of telling me that she didn't understand the question? Was it possible that the portrait of Scoot wasn't even in possession of Tacka Attack Love, but some other unnamed person, who'd either visited or lived in Tokyo, and therefore had been able to access the street and around it where BadDog's creations circulated? Was Her, potentially, murderous?

You anime?

Was I anime?

No. Can you tell me anything else about Her?

You say can anime.

I can anime? I cannot anime.

Sensei? Gakusei?

I didn't know how to explain to Tacka that I didn't understand how she wasn't understanding me. Was Her a sensei? Or an anime? Who did I know with some level of both an English and Japanese acumen that could bridge the gap between myself and the Japanese person I was trying to communicate with?

I messaged Brad.

Sensei was your karate teacher, right?

He responded immediately.

Wtf?
What is gakusei?
Seriously, what drugs are you taking these days?
I responded to Tacka.
I didn't do karate.
Yes, she replied.
No, really. My brother did but he doesn't remember anything about it.
She didn't respond. So I simply just asked, *Do you have the painting?*
After a few moments, she still hadn't answered. Maybe she had travel store again. Or didn't understand the question. What else could I ask her about? DOTA? ASMR?
Her's username? I said.
It was nearing 11:00 in Japan at that point, which meant there were still eighteen hours to go until I'd be eating food at Dan's in Toronto, Canada. I took the egg carton of bean-like cookies out from the fridge. *They weren't that bad,* I told myself. They simply defied expectation. It wasn't like I could make cookies. Or beans. Most importantly, they were here, where other food was not. They almost always were. Because Sarah usually brought a new batch over shortly after I'd thrown the last one out. Crumbs tumbled to the screen where I stared at the conversation with Tacka, still in my hand, still on pause.
I went back again to the photos of Rock Party and tapped the first one in the green-curtained room. It was liked by Tacka Attack Love and fifty-five other people. That was a lot of people. What's more, below the photo, some had added hearts, or flames, or tiny faces that also had colourful mohawks. The second photo was the same. Many, many people liked it, and lots of people expressed this by means of tiny images. It would seem that Rock Party was

some sort of beloved celebrity, at least when they were dressed in what appeared to be their hero costume. To compare, I opened the photo taken in the garden where Rock Party was dressed in their potentially regular outerwear. It had been liked by even more than fifty-five people—211, to be exact, and there were almost an equal amount of hearts, varying in colour and design, below the photo as well. There were even hearts with flames shooting out of them. And also, a note, added by Rock Party, and written in Japanese.

I went back to the first photo in the green-curtained room to see if they'd included one there, too. They hadn't. I checked the second. None. I checked the remaining thirty photos succeeding the garden photo that were taken in the green-curtained room. There were no other notes included by Rock Party. Something was different about the garden photo, beyond costume, setting and crowd response. I checked the date associated with it. August 6. There was no location, no other obvious information. Tapping the photo only resulted in the brief appearance of a heart over Rock Party's drink.

I placed the cookie in my hand back into a cradle of the carton, took the pencil from my ear and went over to the calendar on the wall. I flipped back to August, where I wrote *Rock Party in the garden* on the sixth. Then I noticed the first page of the article from *Japan Views Lifestyle News in English*, tacked directly below the calendar—published, also, on August 6.

I opened Instagram again, this time to look at Tacka's account, at the date the photo of the portrait of the cat identical to Scoot, the cat who could never have even seen his own portrait completed, had been posted. November 10. I wrote this on the calendar, too. Turning back to August, I then wrote *Japan Views Lifestyle News in English article is published* in the same square as *Rock Party in the garden,* as well as in half of the square below that square, around which I added three lines to indicate an extension of the August 6 box, as well as an arrow pointing up. Then I went back to Rock Party's photos and, beginning with the first one, began searching for one that might match the date of Scoot's portrait. The first photo did.

Still no response from Tacka. Did she know what I was doing? Did Dan?

He'd never responded, either.

*

There was no time when I woke up on the floor beside the pencil that must have fallen out from behind my ear, since my phone, no longer in my hand but resting on my stomach, was dead, and also there was little light in the apartment. But what mattered was that there was light. So I got up, placed the phone on the foot of the bed, took off my coat and shoes, went into the washroom, removed the rest of my clothes and took as good a shower as I ever possibly could in what used to be a mop sink. Afterward, I found a change of clothes, potentially clean, in both the drawer beside the kitchenette sink and in the cupboard below that drawer, and dressed there, in the kitchenette, before putting my coat and shoes back on and leaving for Dan's.

Dan lived in a place even more remote than Hadir. It took a subway, a streetcar and a bus to get there, and when I got there I still had to walk fifteen minutes up a hill, one of the only hills in the entire city, so it could have potentially taken a taxi, as well. His house was part of a new development and was attached to a row of other identical houses, four storeys tall and at most two rooms deep, all looking like they were made of plywood then painted the colour of red bricks. Across the street there was another set of the same sort still being built. You could actually see the plywood on those ones, behind their disguise—a semi-translucent curtain with a digitally printed image of the end result on it. But they were nice, regardless. Whenever Dan would open the door for me and I would climb the steps to glimpse my first sight of the super white walls and tiles fabricated to look like hardwood, I would even think, *I would live here.*

This time I thought, *Sarah would live here, too.*

"Nothingness, buddy?" Dan said, looking down at me from the landing. "A little extreme, don't you think? To put that on somebody? Where'd you park?"

"Do you have a phone charger?" I asked him.

"Do you not?"

"Move back so I can be at your level when we talk."

"What?" he said, stepping back inside. I went up the steps and into the house, where Karly's belly, and then face, appeared from around the wall that separated the vestibule from the living room. Her big brown eyes and eyebrows transitioned quickly from worried to happy once she saw my smaller, bluer eyes, and she squeezed her way into the small space, thrusting the dishtowel she'd been holding into Dan's chest.

"Off," she demanded, while unzipping the zipper of my coat and tugging the sleeves from my arms herself. Then she took the coat, pushed Dan backward into the living room and opened the closet he'd been blocking so she could hang it up. Then she turned back around to face me again, clasped her hands, squeezing her own knuckles, until she unclasped them to squeeze my forearms. She was a tiny person, maybe five foot two, so as she led me into the house I felt an instinct to ask Dan why he wasn't holding her now extremely heavy-looking belly for her. Even the big knot of brown hair tied up at the crown of her head seemed like a thing she shouldn't have been carrying around.

"Why you wearing sweats, buddy?" he asked me first.

"Because it's absolutely next-level global-warming freezing out," Karly answered for me, incorrectly. Then to me, she said, "I hate the cold, too."

"I barely notice it," I said.

"You're easygoing, that's why. You're an easygoing person."

Karly was sweet.

"It's not easygoing-ness," Dan said. "Don't encourage him."

"Yes, it is," she said back. "This weather is pure fucking hell. I fucking hate it and I want to move to Bali. Come, Austin. Kitchen. Would you like a sandwich?"

"Yeah, why are you here at two in the afternoon?" Dan said.

Two pm. Fourteen hundred hours. I'd slept through the entire afternoon and evening in Japan.

"Do you have a phone charger?" I asked him again.

"Why were you texting Brad weird shit about karate?" he asked.

"There's one in the kitchen," Karly said, while pulling on what felt like my abnormally large hand when being held by hers. At first I didn't move, because I was still looking at Dan who was looking at me, but on the second, more assertive tug, I did. He followed behind us, clapping both of his even-larger-than-mine hands on my shoulders and massaging. Between the two of them, I felt completely disassociated from any sense of my own size, until I was sat down in a chair where they finally let me go. There were white flowers in a glass vase on the table right beside me. I could smell them.

"How did you get these flowers in the winter?" I said.

"Are you serious?" said Dan.

"You notice everything, Austin. There's a new grocery store over there that's like, Euro-style." She waved at the back door, then took a phone charger out from a glass cabinet full of more phone chargers, as well as beautiful white plates, and placed it in my hand like it was a treasure, sort of folding my fingers over it, then cupping my fist. "More like a market, really. Like in Europe. Keep it. We have a hundred."

"Now you're enabling," said Dan. "You can't keep that."

"Dan," Karly yelled.

"Well, he can't," Dan yelled back.

I bent over my knees to plug it into the wall outlet beneath my chair. Next, I needed the password for Dan's Wi-Fi.

"Are you feeling faint? Why are you bent over like that?" he yelled at me.

I sat up.

"When was the last time you ate?" he said.

"I'm not faint."

"Don't make him a sandwich," he yelled at Karly. "This is ridiculous. Dinner's not enough. It never is. You still have to take whatever else you can squeeze out of me. Like I don't have my own kid to be thinking about here?"

"I'm not faint," I repeated.

Karly yelled, "Dan, it's nice that he came early. It's nice to have more time."

Dan: "He didn't even let us know he was coming early."

Karly: "His phone was dead."

Dan: "Why doesn't he have a charger?"

Karly: "Not everyone does. God."

Then Karly sat down in a chair. But that didn't seem to matter to Dan.

"I'm the one who always wanted more time. Literally, always suggesting more time. But it never seemed to matter to him." He turned to me. "You don't check in with anyone unless it's for some completely random reason, you don't show up unless you need something, and I always give you whatever it is, no matter what it is, that you need. I got you that phone and you don't even take care of it."

"How do you take care of a phone?" I said.

"Charge it," he yelled.

"I am."

"How are you paying the bill for it? How are you paying your rent, even?"

Clearly I'd have to wait for a moment alone with Karly to ask for the Wi-Fi password.

"Don't make him a sandwich, Karly," he said. "Don't give him any money. If he doesn't want to grow up, fine, but I'm not going to keep helping him when it does nothing, apparently. He doesn't appreciate it. He doesn't appreciate anything we've already done. Because you did it all for him too, Karly. Because, what's mine is yours, and our future family's, so you're getting taken for granted, too. You're being victimized, too. And that's what he needs to hear. That he's hurt you, not me. I can handle it. I'm his brother. I have to. But Karly, she didn't ask for you to treat her like this."

"Treat her how?"

"Like you don't appreciate everything she's done for you."

This was all Hadir's fault. I looked over at Karly. "I'm sorry about school."

"Austin, I don't—"

"She's not going to tell you she cares," said Dan.

"I'm going to be coming into much reward soon," I said. "I don't know how much exactly, but I'll pay back the baby—"

"The baby?" yelled Dan.

"You just said—"

"This isn't about money," he yelled.

"Then what is it about?"

"You. Thinking you're going to win the lottery, or whatever the fuck you're talking about. You have issues, and the next thing, I know it, is going to be you calling from a freaking hospital, or the parking lot of a Walmart, saying you've been evicted, again, and you're sleeping in your fucking car, again, and your phone's almost dead because you have no fucking charger."

I stood up and the cord detached from the phone. I'd need more of a charge than that, but I also couldn't stay in the room any longer. Dan had succeeded in that way, in making me want to leave. He said more things, still, as I walked back through the living room and up the stairs to the second-floor washroom, but I willed them to the place where I couldn't hear them anymore.

The room across from the washroom on the second floor was a nursery. I hadn't seen it before. I'd never seen any nursery before, actually. It was painted the colour of a pistachio, and there was a wooden crib, and a dresser with a mat on it, and a box of diapers, and a basket stuffed with a bunch of animals. I went inside, crouched down beside the basket, and picked out a soft brown squirrel. There were also two shelves on the wall in front of me, one with block letters set up to spell the word *BABY*, and the other with space to be filled with things accrued throughout said baby's eventual life, I guessed.

I heard footsteps up the stairs. It was Karly. She came into the nursery.

"There's an outlet by the dresser," she said, plugging in the phone charger. Then came to take my phone. "Oh, yeah. That squirrel. Muriel gave that to me."

I didn't know who Muriel was.

"How did you manage to bring the phone charger up here without Dan yelling a bunch?"

"He did. You didn't hear?"

I was better at willing than I thought. After plugging in my phone, Karly went to the closet and pulled out a very tiny tuxedo.

"Look," she said. "Look at how weird this is."

"Are you having a boy?"

"I don't know. I don't think so."

She brought it over and sat down on the other side of the basket where she took out a badger and started dressing it.

"You know, for some reason, I feel like I can't age," she said. "I mean, I can get a wrinkle or a grey hair or whatever, but I can't seem to accomplish that transition from young woman to woman. Even though I'm pregnant. You know? Sometimes, I'm just like, 'I'm twelve years old. How will I birth and raise this baby? What is wrong with me?'"

I bet Dan never asked what was wrong with himself.

"Wasn't there a time when it was commonplace for twelve-year-olds to become pregnant?" I said.

"Like, medieval times?"

"Yes."

"I don't know. But I was sad to hear about your cat."

"Thanks," I said.

"That's why I wanted you to come over."

"Because the cat?"

"I had a rabbit when I was kid."

Were we having rabbit for dinner?

"Are you feeling a bit better? Now that a couple of days have passed?"

The thing about Karly was that, even though she was right, and she did come across particularly youthful, she still had a Master of Science degree and ran her own psychotherapy clinic.

"I'm still really sad," I said.

She nodded while kind of petting the badger's head.

"And, something weird is going on," I continued.

"What is it?" she said.

How was I supposed to explain this without showing her the wall?

"Have you ever had a client who claimed to be an animalist?"

"As in, a person who believes they're an animal?"

"Is that the definition of an animalist?"

"Like, basically."

I needed to write that down.

"Can I ask you, Karly, do you have Wi-Fi, and also paper and a pencil?"

"I think I have a card around here. Help me?"

I stood up from the floor, then helped Karly up, too. From one of the dresser drawers she withdrew a business card and pen, both upon which her name was inscribed. "And it's Drizzynet," she said. "The Wi-Fi. The password's Dan's phone number."

I copied down her definition of an animalist while she undressed the badger.

"Dan'll be pissed if he sees this," she said, regarding the tuxedo. "Kev gave it to us." She stuck out her tongue. "Kev."

"Have you ever thought about moving to a plot of land?" I asked her.

"And like, building a house?"

"Maybe. Or maybe there's already a house there. And you could raise the baby a safe distance from all of the animalists of the city."

"My office is in the city."

"You could open a new office on a plot of land, one full of areas to garden. Lots of people find gardening to be therapeutic."

"I mean, it's a good idea, in theory. But we'd be too far away from you. I wouldn't like that." She hung the tuxedo back up in the closet, then chucked the badger at the basket. It didn't go in. "Plus, there'd be animals there, too. Come downstairs when you're ready."

I waited until she'd left the room, then went and picked up the badger, and placed it in the crib. I didn't want to explain to Karly that travelling by a single train to the nearest neighbouring farming town took less time than it did to reach her current house by any combination of inner-city transit vehicles, because I didn't want her to do something like call me a taxi, or worse, ask Dan to give me a ride back to my apartment later. But I did want to explain one more thing to her before she was all the way downstairs. So I unplugged the charger from the wall with the phone still attached to it, and sprinted from the room.

"I'm going to be a very conscientious uncle," I whispered down to her.

She stopped on the steps and looked back up to me.

"Aw. One sec." Then she turned around and climbed back up. At the top, she pet my arm, and then her own belly. "Put the charger in your sweater pocket," she said.

*

Dan was in the kitchen doing something on his own phone.

"Get a drink and go chill in the living room," he said, without looking up. The idea crossed my mind to simply tell him everything, about the painting, Instagram, Walmart, ASMR. But he was too busy. He didn't even notice when I waved my hand in front of his face. So I did get a glass bottle of Italian mineral water from the fridge, then went into the living room. Karly started cooking. I could hear that, for a while, neither of them were speaking. It was funny how the same two people dressed up like rich celebrities wearing Santa hats and posed on a bed covered in red satin sheets in the framed photograph displayed above the couch could be the same two people who were just yelling at each other over a phone charger.

I took the charger out of my pocket and swapped it out with the plug for the lamp, then connected to Dan's Wi-Fi. Still no message from Tacka. Maybe she was feeling stalked, after all.

Dan came into the living room.

"We can eat now. Why are you on the floor?"

"It's not dinnertime, is it?"

"No, Austin, but you came here at two in the afternoon and you look homeless. So we're going to eat now."

"I'm not homeless."

"I know, I pay your rent."

"My savings pays my rent."

"You have savings because you quit school and took all the money I gave you for tuition and textbooks and then tried to hide it from me, and lied to me—"

"Shut up, Dan," Karly yelled from the kitchen. He held out a hand to help me up. I didn't take it. I didn't stand up, either.

"Dan, something weird is going on," I said.

"This is just you. It's who you are. I get it."

"It's not me. It's BadDog."

His phone vibrated in his other hand. He looked at it and went, "Ha," then started typing on it again. "You're my youngest brother," he said.

And?

"And I live with a therapist, buddy. I think I know a bit more about your motives than you do."

How could he think up things like that to say to me while typing other things to someone else on his phone at the same time?

"My only motive is to get a clear answer from Tacka Attack Love concerning the identity of the possessor of the portrait in the photograph. At this moment, anyway."

Dan looked up from his phone to the wall above the couch. Then back down to his phone, and continued typing. "That? We're gonna take a new one with the baby. Dressed like a roast chicken? It doesn't make any sense."

"Yes it does," I said.

From the kitchen, Karly yelled, "What about it doesn't make sense?"

Dan: "Are you kidding?"

Me: "How do you convince someone you aren't stalking them?"

Karly: "What kind of creeps just place a baby in the middle of a table set with a bunch of food, when it's not even dressed like a food itself? Like, what are you implying?"

*

AN AXOLOTL

Even though when he first moved to Canada and didn't know anyone, and was still learning English, and I was the only person who would offer to pair up with him for gym, or reading, and I'd bring cool figurines over to his house to show him, and then, still, in high school, when I didn't even go anymore, meet up with him after class, even though to anyone who saw us together he would refer to me as his volunteering hours, or his sad loner orphan friend, and even though he had a habit of hitting me upside the head in public, and sucking his braces like they were grills, and clearly had no respect for my personal boundaries with Dan, it was the way in which Hadir had, in the past, mocked Sarah's most beautiful outfits that bothered me the most. Why did he have to drag her into anything? She was the last person in the world who deserved to be ridiculed for any reason whatsoever, let alone her style, which was both cool and exquisite. Was he even aware of all of this? Should I write this all down in a letter and deliver it to him, then leave just before he reads it? Or, stay while he reads it? Or, I could give it to Hadir's dad to deliver to Hadir for me.

"I sympathize with you," Sarah said, taking the latte she'd brought over from my hands and setting it on the floor between us, because with all of the remembering and not-paying-attention-to-the-present I was doing, I'd kept nearly letting it spill over. "But I wouldn't bother with a letter."

She was right. Not only would his dad simply read it aloud, laugh at me and then throw it in the compost instead of passing it on to Hadir anyway, but Hadir's connection to Tacka, as much as I didn't want it to be, might still prove useful. Sarah sighed, and nodded, like she was thinking the exact same thing. Or like she was thinking about the job she didn't get because of the nearly one hundred other candidates with resumés that included recent typing experience on a computer that was not their own personal device.

"Yep," she said.

"What are you thinking about?" I tried to clarify.

"Proposing to Aisopos that I repaint the kitchen cupboards in exchange for my share of the utilities bills for next month." She was studying the pictures on Rock Party's Instagram account. "Have you noticed the bit of table in the curtained-room photos?" she said.

"Yes."

"It's an odd table. Thin. More like a tray. What kind of room would have a tray-like table in it? Wait." She tapped at my phone, then turned it toward me. "Look."

It was the portrait of Scoot again. I turned my face away, to the edge of the bed right beside her.

"Not at the cat. Look at the picture," Sarah said, placing the phone in my hand, moving my hand up to my face, then turning my face to my hand. "Look at the table the picture is on."

I did. It was the same as it was before. So I moved my hand to the side and looked into Sarah's eyes to try and read her mind. Her pupils were sparkly, and her also sparkly aquamarine eyeliner was really pretty that night. She smiled.

"It's the same colour as the one in the green-curtained room," I realized. Then I went back to Rock Party's profile and tapped the first picture and zoomed in on the table. The more I zoomed in, the fuzzier the table became, but in that fuzz there was no denying what could quite possibly be one half of a crescent stain most likely created by the bottom of a wet cup. Sarah made a fist and struck it against the floor, once, then lifted the latte to my mouth.

"Sip," she said. "You're on to something."

CHAPTER 6

Another New Key

I whistled gently so the sheet of paper on top of the books on top of the box of more paper that I was holding with both of my arms would flutter to the counter, showing Grear what I'd written. She put on her glasses and looked it over, then set the paper to the side.

"That's almost all of what it says. Or, what it might say, in the note below the photograph of Rock Party in the garden. I'm pretty sure it begins with the letters T and A, and thus may be saying something about tapestry. Or tablespoons. What this has to do with Neofinetia orchids, I do not know. Yet. There is a connection. It could also be about shoes, like a type of new, and very stylish athletic shoe, for tennis, or tap dancing, even, but I think that's less likely the case. Unless tap dancing is hyphenated, in which case I'd have to figure out if there is a character somewhere in the three types of Japanese writing systems that translates to the concept of a hyphen, as well as when, how, and if it was employed by Rock Party in said note, but again, my gut says no, it's not about the shoes."

"Guts always know."

Wise. I tilted the box so that the books would fall to the counter next. "Here I have one dictionary to translate Japanese to English, and another to translate Japanese characters to Roman. And this is a box of paper, the kind where all the sheets are attached like toilet paper, and you have to be very gentle when separating them, and then you have to tear the edges with all the holes off after, too. It's from Aisopos's house. He'd been storing it in the cold room. We don't know why he had them. Sarah tried to find out, but she said he acted like he'd never even known there was a cold room in the first place. I cannot corroborate this. I was waiting outside when it happened." I bent my leg so as to balance the box on one knee and free a hand to remove my phone from my pocket. I opened the Instagram app. "Is your internet working?"

"No," said Grear.

"That's okay," I said, putting the phone away. "I copied down the note, just in case." I untucked the box flaps, lifted the top sheet to carefully separate it from the next, then blew the comment written by Rock Party beneath their thirty-third most recent Instagram post, as replicated by me, with a pencil, to the counter. "I'll tear the edges off, after."

Grear traced over the letters with one half of my broken key.

"It's a multi-step process to translate," I said. "Hence the multiple books. And my uncertainty of the translating I've done so far."

"I like puzzles," Grear said. "I can help."

"Can I add translation services to my tab?"

"I like puzzles," she said again. "Go sit. Billy been stabbed leaving the courthouse. It's all taped."

I went around the counter and set the box down on the removable van seat. Grear turned on the television, where a newscast transitioned to a *CSI* episode. As the two scenes were interposed between one another, the image on the screen blended into one dead body. I picked up the box again.

"I'll be taping over it soon," she said.

"I need to watch this right now," I replied, regarding the paper on the counter. For all I knew, Grear was about to play an imperative role in the unanticipated storyline of my own life, unearthing, potentially, a translation not at all related to tap dance, tap dancing, or anything basically harmless. What could be lurking in this Japanese garden? Which, if any, ominous words began with the phonemes T and A?

Grear opened one of the books to a Battleship grid of Hiragana, Katakana and Roman letter blends. I tore another sheet from the box, and she pulled a pencil from her hair bun.

"Taxidermy," I said. Grear paused without lifting the pencil from the page, and looked up at me without pushing her glasses up the bridge of her nose. "The art of stuffing animal skins."

She stood up straight from the counter, then spun the paper 180 degrees beneath the lead of the pencil.

"Aha," she said.

"Aha? Is that a good interjection? Or a frightened one?"

She tapped the pencil against the paper three times. *Tapioca next life*. Then she closed the book and faultlessly tore the edges from the paper in one fell tug. "I like puzzles, and I am good at them."

After that, Grear cut me a new key.

*

What I'd quickly come to realize first about the twenty-four-hour tapioca juice restaurant one block west and two more south of Grear's hardware store, was that it posted its customer Wi-Fi password by the bathroom door, so all I had to do was walk inside, ask the server at the counter for a cup of tap water and then hold that cup of tap water out in front of me so as to let it remain visible while I walked to the washroom to connect to BubbleHeaven2. Once connected, I could go back to the dining area and take a seat on the purple bench of the yellow-tabled booth, which I'd claimed upon entry by way of setting atop my new box of old papers, two books, re-creation of Rock Party's note, Grear's translation of it and the three packs of instant ramen noodles she'd sent me away with.

Which was, as it turned out, a smart thing to do, because what I'd quickly come to realize second about the twenty-four-hour tapioca juice restaurant one block west and two more south of the building where I lived, was that at exactly 21:00, it turned into a party. The lights changed from normal to off to technicolour disco ball, and three consecutive groups of ten college students packed themselves into the narrow yet long space, sitting in booths, standing in doubles, or clusters, or circles just outside the front door, vaping, and sucking up little black beads from their multi-coloured milks. Some had even brought their own refillable, bedazzled cups, personalized with miniature charms looped where the base of the straw entered the detachable lids via a hole cut into the hard plastic. What was in this juice that had these kids choosing it over something like alcohol, or energy drinks, or regular juice, even? I was afraid to find out. And also, had no way of doing so without Sarah or Dan around to lend me some money. I was entirely out.

A young woman in a dress that matched the disco ball appeared beside my booth.

"Hi," she said, which I assumed meant she wanted to sit down.

"Sure," I said.

I was right. She tossed her coat to the other side of the bench and placed her violet-coloured drink on the table, then sat close enough to the edge of the booth so that her ankles could cross off to the side.

"I'm Matilda. I'm here with those guys, but I wanted to come say hi. Hi."

Those guys could have been any of the thirty people in or around the restaurant. Or all of them.

"I'm Austin," I said.

"Are you a beaver?"

No, obviously not, Matilda.

"Do I look like one?"

"Mm," she said, crossing her ankles the other way. "Good point. No. You don't. Where do you go?"

"All over the city, it seems."

Which also didn't seem to answer Matilda's question. But what I did like about talking to her was that she moved on with things, and people like that don't take too long to get through a conversation with when you need to get back to parsing out meaning from a partially translated note.

"What's your major?" she asked.

"It was Media Arts and Animation. I changed it to nothing a few months ago."

"What are you working on then?"

"The articles, and possibly adverbs. Yours?"

"Economics. Pre-law. Pre-Chief Justice of Canada."

She twirled her straw. Its charm jingled. A little silver bell. She pointed the tip in my direction. "Sip?"

I looked around the restaurant, at all the people who didn't seem to see the two of us sitting there. Had she actually arrived with anyone else? Had anyone? Was anyone else sharing drinks? I leaned forward and let her place the straw in my mouth. Just the plastic alone, with its mix of leftover droplets and ChapStick, was delicious. What was that flavour? Upon full first sample, my entire head tingled.

"Did this drink just do ASMR to me?" I said.

"Maybe. Want some more?"

My phone began to ring. I took it from my pocket. It was Brad.

"Austin," he yelled, as if he were in the restaurant with me. "Where are you? Are you at a club?"

"Is this a club?" I asked Matilda.

"No." She smiled.

"How are the girls?" said Brad.

"Kind, it seems. And ambitious. Though potentially beguiling."

"Ha," Brad laughed. "I need the car."

"Did I just take some kind of communion?"

"Are you talking to me?" Matilda said.

"Are these charms a sort of token one earns for acquiring new members?"

Matilda giggled, fondling the silver bell. She was reminding me a lot of the kaftan man at that moment, with her head cocked, and lips pouted, while offering me more to drink. I needed to get off the phone with Brad. I needed to see the photo of Rock Party in the garden again.

"I have to go," I said.

"Can I pick it up tomorrow?"

"I don't have it," I said.

"Does Kirk?"

"No. Christiansen."

"Who the fuck is Christiansen?"

"The person from Craigslist. First name R."

"You sold the car?"

This was taking forever.

"I need my phone for other reasons right now, Brad. Please try again later."

I ended the call and opened the Instagram app to Rock Party's photos. Matilda watched while drinking her drink. I zoomed in on the cup in Rock Party's hand, where the almost entirely unnoticeable balls of a small chain, the likes of which would likely be looped through a charm dangling off the side of the rim and facing inward toward Rock Party's chest, were wrapped around the base of the straw. The straw connected to a metallic lid tinted silver—a fact neither Sarah nor myself had previously noticed, or noted as such, probably due to there being so much to note about the photo already.

I went to Tacka's photos next and opened the most recent one of herself plus two friends sipping drinks from straws. Three charms, one clear glass bead shaped like a pebble, one bronze coin and one white glass cat, hung from three varied cups—a teal cup with diamonds encircling the lip, a metallic cup tinted gold and a metallic cup tinted silver. Rock Party's. These personalized cups were intercontinental. As were these charms, and this bewitching juice, and Matilda, Tacka and Rock Party were all involved in their promotion. I zoomed in on the charm of the white cat that hung from Rock Party's cup. Its eyes appeared to be either closed or non-existent. One front paw appeared to be either tucked inward, or half-missing. It appeared to either be any cat, or Scoot. I whistled.

"Can I try another sip of your drink?" I asked Matilda, whose head was still cocked. Her hair was cut in a very straight line right beneath her ear. Some had fallen in front of her lips and gotten stuck in the corner of them. She leaned over the table, straw pinched between her fingertips. They gently brushed my lips as she placed it upon them.

"You're kind of weird," she said.

It was potato and vanilla.

"Could I borrow a sheet?" she asked.

I opened the box of Aisopos's old paper and separated a sheet for her. She reached over and took the pencil from my ear, shielded the paper from my view as she wrote, then folded it over on itself several times until it took the shape of something else.

"If you want to try a different flavour sometime," she said as she slid the shape across the table. Then she leaned over and slipped the pencil back behind my ear, stood from the booth and disappeared into the crowd, leaving me with goosebumps and an origami cat that fit perfectly into a card slot of my empty wallet.

*

It had been twenty-three days since a cat worth a reward potentially very large in sum and identical to the subject of a painting, and now, possibly, a glass charm, too, had appeared at the foot of my door—a cat that may have been stolen and transported all the way from Japan by an individual, or a group of people who believe they are animals, or who steal animals from people who believe they are animals and who, for reasons still unclear, are using said animals. They were doing this to either send a message regarding an impending violent takeover of their animalistic organization, or to frame urban civilians, at random, or in specific, as murderers, in order to claim the sums of very large rewards for themselves, by placing said animals in front of said civilian doors, of which mine was one, and of whom I let in, deloused, adopted and loved within a matter of hours, or less.

Now, three weeks and two days later, I found myself, consequently, sitting on the floor of my apartment, holding a guitar I couldn't even play properly, because I'd sold the corresponding amplifier one week prior to the same guy who took the car. I stared up at a work of deconstructed origami fabricated with fax paper older than I was that had a ten-digit phone number pencilled across it, and which had been tacked to my wall next to an attempted translation of an attempted replication of a phrase originally typed in Japanese, then written in pencil onto fax paper and tacked beside the definition of an animalist, as defined by Karly, a therapist, and copied by myself onto the back of one her business cards, which was tacked above a Wikipedia entry on ASMR, as well as the visitor information page for the Missouri Botanical Gardens. I was trying to figure out what, if anything, I, Austin, could do to obtain the sum being offered for my dead pet, while preventing any more messages, framings or murders in the process.

Was there another group of people? Perhaps even civilians who had, themselves, received a message in some form, and who were now organizing themselves against the takeover? Of which Tacka, Her, Matilda and Rock Party were all members? With the charms displayed on the cups of their tapioca juice being some sort of silent indication of such membership to the others? What did the orchids indicate? Was Aisopos a member of this group? Those were technically his plants Sarah so dutifully cared for, and it was technically his doorstep upon which the fish she'd ended up adopting had been placed.

I separated a new sheet of Aisopos's paper and wrote *Aisopos* on it, then tacked it to the wall. Then, I laid the guitar on its back and removed each string. One string I coiled around the two thumbtacks pinning each the origami cat, representative of Matilda, and the pencilled addendum originally written by Rock Party beneath their photo. Another string linked the cat to the tack tacking the Wikipedia information on ASMR, representing Tacka Attack Love, and one more connected ASMR to the Missouri Botanical Gardens, home of the Neofinetia orchid collection. A fourth string I then strung from the Missouri Botanical Gardens to the name Aisopos. I took a step back. Of course, Sarah had been right. A perfect zigzag had been revealed.

On another sheet of paper I wrote *BubbleHeaven2* and tacked it right in the centre of everything else. Up to this moment, it had seemed that Tacka Attack Love and her Instagram account were the bridge connecting Japan to North America. But perhaps, in fact, it was tapioca juice, or more specifically, tapioca juice straws, and most importantly, the personalized charms that dangled from the base of the straws that were, in fact, bridges. In which case, the origami cat, Rock Party's partially translated text and the ASMR information could all be moved to the outside frame, and still connect to the middle. But what about Aisopos, and the Missouri Botanical Gardens?

Have travel store have cut hair
Tacka.
sorry so.
You don't have to say sorry, I responded.
Her you find west the park. MAU. Her do Instagram no.
Mau? Was that Her's name?
You do not find her on Instagram? I asked.
No. No.
What?
What do you mean by the second No?
Do painting.

She didn't do the painting. I knew that.
Does Rock Party have the painting on their table?
No response.
Is Rock Party Her?
Her Tokyo.
Where is Rock Party?
Hospital Fukuoka. Have cut hair.
Another haircut?
"Wait," I said aloud as I messaged her to wait.
OK, she said.
Is there tapioca juice at the hospital?
Have hospital I give tapioca juice.

Then she said, *Mm.* Then, sent a picture of a green heart, all of which I supposed meant that she thought green tapioca juice was good. Or, green like a garden, where she might drink the juice through a charmed straw, with Rock Party, while taking their picture for them. So, perhaps what Tacka Attack Love actually meant by her use of "to have" was "to go." *Go* travel to a store. *Go* to a haircut. *Go* to the hospital and give tapioca juice to Rock Party in the garden. It made sense, since you still might *have* to go to a store, or *have* a haircut scheduled.

But then, what was meant by the word "do"? Have? Her does not *do* Instagram, thus her does not *have* an account? So, "do painting'" would equal "have painting"? Which would mean Tacka does not *have* the painting, and it would make no sense to her why I would ask if Rock Party *go* the painting on their table, which would explain the figurative blank stare in response. Tacka Attack Love was simply not clear on how auxiliary verbs worked.

Are you still there, Tacka?
OK.

Rock Party do the painting of the cat?
Yes.
Now we were getting somewhere.
Why does Rock Party do the painting? Who gives it to them at Hospital Fukuoka?
Have hospital gives painting.
You gave it to Rocky Party?
Yes. You guitar online?
Did BadDog give the painting to you?
Her.
So Her must know BadDog.
Silence. I had to figure out what "must" was.
Her might know BadDog.
Her may know BadDog.
Her should know BadDog.
Yes, she said.
"Should" equalled "must."
Who is Her?
Who could Her?
Who shall Her?
Who am Her?
Is sister.
"Is" was "is."
Your sister?
Yes.
I immediately separated a sheet of Aisopos's paper and wrote *Her* on it, tacked it above the biography of BadDog as included on the contest website, and, with the final string, connected the two via the tack of "ASMR."

Do you know where Missouri is? I asked Tacka next, but to this, and so many more questions that still remained, I did not receive an answer. Why did Her give her sister this painting? Why did Tacka then give the painting to Rock Party? Why would Tacka be the one to create a picture of the painting on Instagram instead of Rock Party, and why did she also create the picture of the orchid identical to Aisopos's, as well as those featured at the Missouri Botanical Gardens in Missouri, the same state where the manufacturer of the treats that the real cat depicted in the painting enjoyed eating for the brief but significant time he was the adopted pet of myself, friend of the girl who cared for said orchid identical to the one in said picture, and who was with me in both the moment the photo was posted, and when the treats were purchased? What happened on November the tenth?

Again, I took the treats out from the nightstand drawer. They were the very last thing I'd purchased on my own with the final bit of money I had left from the car. I'd never actually shook them before, as suggested. What was the point? It just sounded like food things in a package being tossed around. Like pasta noodles in a box in a grocery basket as you walked. Or croutons in a box in a grocery basket as you walked. Those are not sounds that make me excited to eat pasta or croutons. Did the pet food manufacturers in Missouri think cats were stupid? When I offered them to Scoot, I'd open the package and hold it within smelling range. It's smell that makes you excited to eat. Not annoying rhythms and overly colourful packaging with the words *Party Mix* stamped across the front.

Party Mix.

Stupidity.

Cheesy fingerprints on the back of the packaging.

I took the treats to the wall and pinned them to the left of everything else. Stupid, corrupt Yvette, manager-on-duty and friend of the disturbing kaftan-slash-sportswear-clad squatter living in the pet section at the Walmart where Aisopos purchased his orchid—an orchid identical to the orchids on display at the Missouri Botanical Gardens, as well as to that which was depicted by Tacka Attack Love in photographic form for Sarah—the former stock clerk (whom the squatter had gotten fired) and caretaker of the original orchid—to see. Yvette, manager-on-duty of the same Walmart where I, Austin, purchased litter, a tray, cougar food and the treats manufactured in Missouri for the cat identical to the subject of the painting also depicted as a photograph by Tacka Attack Love for Hadir, childhood and now untrustworthy best friend of I, Austin, to see. Manager-on-duty who, as Sarah (who could likely be trusted) claimed, was always eating Party Mix. If I had any more string in that moment, I would have connected the package of treats to the Missouri Botanical Gardens via Karly's business card definition of an animalist, which would have served to represent the kaftan man, and which would have connected to the connection already made between the Gardens and Aisopos. But I didn't. So I had to imagine one was there, and in doing so, it became apparent that there was but one missing link to BubbleHeaven2.

If you aren't awake now, we need to talk when you are.

Aisopos. Was he actually aware of what was going on when we took the box of paper? And by acting like he wasn't, was he, in all actuality, helping us?

The phone rang.

"The longer I go without a job, the later into the night I stay awake. I don't like this," said Sarah.

"I'm sorry."

"I like waking up early. I like showering first thing and going out. I like carrying a thermos of coffee and a container with cookies in it to a place where I have to go."

I could tell things were starting to catch up to her. It made me resent the kaftan man even more.

"What do you need to talk to me about?" she said.

"I need to have a conversation with Aisopos. I think he knows more than he's letting on."

"He definitely knows more than he lets on. He watches the local news every evening. I've heard him speak to the neighbours."

"Not about the English language, but also, yes, that's part of what I'm referring to. What I mean is, I think he knows more about other things."

Sarah was quiet.

"So, I'll come over tomorrow. We'll also need more string, and tapioca juice. And new guitar strings, because without them, I won't get as much for the guitar as I otherwise could."

Another moment passed. She still hadn't said anything.

"It's, like, a fifty-dollar difference at the pawnshop," I said.

"Austin, there's a job fair at a new restaurant opening in Liberty Village tomorrow, and after that I was planning to disseminate resumes door-to-door."

"Have you ever noticed Aisopos carrying around, or possibly even wearing a charm of some sort? Particularly one made of white glass and shaped like a cat?"

"No. Why?"

"The fish was on Aisopos's doorstep. You fertilized his orchid the day that Scoot showed up. I can build the outside of the puzzle first, but I need to connect Aisopos to the middle."

"Are you saying that you think Aisopos has something to do with the painting? Or, that I may have something to do with the painting?"

"I'm saying, I think Aisopos knew we would need this paper. He might have even known Scoot was going to arrive, some place, at some point, after the fish, and on a day that you were scheduled to fertilize his orchid."

Again, Sarah was quiet.

"Are you working on your resume right now?" I asked her.

"I think Aisopos is a very old man. And I think someone just didn't want that fish anymore. I know it's hard to believe, but people can just give up like that. On fish."

Maybe things were more than just catching up to Sarah. It sounded like she needed a latte.

"We can always have tapioca juice and lattes," I said. "And I swear, once I sell this guitar, solve this mystery and claim much reward before some other nefarious character does, they'll both be on me."

"I believe you about things, Austin. But I don't want my fish to be involved."

I knew that. Even in bringing it up then, I knew that. After the weeping, after she'd let go of me on her own, because I didn't want to be the one to suggest it was ever the time for her to do so, Sarah didn't even want to place a rock over that fish's grave. She didn't even want to make a mark on the ground with a stick. She stepped on the dirt to make it look less freshly turned-up, and then ground away the footprint.

"I'll be there first thing in the morning," I said. "You won't miss the fair."

I needed to sell that guitar.

CHAPTER 7

An Interview with Aisopos

Sarah directed me to a foldable dining chair she'd set up on one side of a coffee table that Aisopos was already on the other side of, on a sofa, eating a sandwich. Another sandwich, set upon a little white saucer on the table, she then gave to me. She wasn't dressed; in fact, she was wearing a very fluffy yellow robe over top of her bare legs, with matching fluffy yellow slippers on her feet, which was a side of her I really liked to see. While Aisopos did nod as I took a bite of the sandwich, as though affirming on my behalf that Sarah's bologna, mustard and cheese was, without a doubt, excellent, he certainly did not appear to see me sitting there, as he had yet to look away from the morning show on the television screen beside me. Sarah leaned a didgeridoo against his arm of the couch, then stood in front of the screen and placed her hand on my shoulder.

"Austin is going to chit-chat with you now while I get ready for my job interview. He's nice to talk with. You can knock if you need me."

At this, Aisopos did not nod, only tried to look around her.

"He needs to knock if he needs anything," she said to me. Then she left through the kitchen to her bedroom on the other side. I set the saucer on the floor beside my chair, took a sheet of paper from the pillowcase in my lap, and the pencil from behind my ear.

"Sarah tells me you have a Neofinetia?" I started.

Aisopos shook his head no. He had a happy-looking smile, though. Whether it was because of my company, or the morning show host with hair like waves of milk chocolate flowing down the spout of a mixer and onto a conveyor belt to be tempered, I wasn't sure, but I surely felt more comfortable pressing on in response to it.

"An orchid. With skinny white petals that fan out like a firework."

Again, a no. But his smile grew.

"Maybe the best thing would be to start at the beginning. Where did you come from, and how did you wind up here, in this house, a relatively short distance away from the Walmart in question—the question being that which we'll get to later, when we get closer to the latter half of things?"

He looked away from the screen then, to the sandwich in his hand. Then, for the first time, he looked at me, while raising the sandwich as if it were a glass. I raised mine, too. I supposed we were toasting Sarah then, for the gesture, but also, in a way, for her many constant gestures, and that was how I knew that Aisopos and I were officially communicating.

"Cool," he said with a nod.

"Yes, cool," I replied. Following his lead, I took another bite, and then Aisopos set his sandwich down on the sofa. He partially pulled himself up to stand with the didgeridoo, then with a few sideways steps seated himself in the wheelchair that was parked beside the sofa. He pointed to the other side of the room, to a cabinet with two glass panes set in the corner beside the window. I placed my sandwich on its saucer, folded the paper into my back pocket, stuck my pencil back behind my ear and went to push him in that direction. In front of the cabinet, he reached over the chair and tugged my sleeve.

"You want me to get something from there?"

"Yep," he said.

"Okay." I went in front of him to open the two panes. Not knowing which object he was referring to, I picked up the first thing from the leftmost corner of the top left shelf—a small yet heavy silver chicken nest, with a chicken in it, sitting on some eggs.

"What's this for?" I said.

He made a motion for me to hand it to him. I did. He held it with one hand and plopped it into the palm of the other, a few times, at least, while his mouth smiled, dropped and smiled again, as if his facial muscles were attached to the chicken by fishing wire. He handed it back to me, and I plopped it into one palm, too. Something about its plop-ability, its weight, seemed important. I set it back in its spot on the shelf and took the paper from my pocket, pencil from my ear and wrote *heavy chicken*. Aisopos pointed at the top left shelf again, so I took out the next object. A small brass swan.

"Why all the fowl, Aisopos?" I asked him.

"Greece," he said. Then he pointed to the right side of the cabinet. I picked out the first object from the top right shelf—a porcelain pot with a countryside scene painted on it. I handed it to Aisopos. He held it on his lap, tapping the simple red house beneath a yellow-leaved tree.

"Was that your house?" I asked him.

"Yep," he said. Then tapped the pond next to the house.

"And pond?"

"Yep."

"There were swans in the pond?"

"Yep."

"And chickens around the house?"

"Yep."

So Aisopos came from a bird farm in Greece.

"And what brought you to Toronto?"

He pointed back up to the shelf, to a statuette that looked like a werewolf carved from some kind of dark wood propped next to the empty space where the pot had been. On the other side of the statue was an old photograph of a young man no older than I was, and a younger boy. Aisopos signalled vigorously for me to hand him the picture.

"Father," he said, pointing at the man. Then, at the boy: "Aisopos." He rubbed his thumb and fingers together. "Father," he said, "*putanas yos*. Gambler. Trouble with the Wolfman on Fylis Street." He gave the picture back to me. Then he pointed to a die on the second shelf below. I set the picture back in its spot, picked up the die and turned it over in my hand. Each side was marked with a symbol I assumed were the Greek numerals one through six.

"One through six?" I confirmed.

He opened his palm for me to place it upon.

"When the Wolfman came, he rolled the die, my father." Aisopos rotated the die to a blue F-looking thing. "His first roll, digamma. So the Wolfman left. Next day he came again, and again, he rolled it. My father."

Then he handed the die to me and waved, as if to say, *Go on and do something with it*. So I threw it on the floor. It rolled under his chair. I crouched down to see which side it had landed on. That blue F-looking thing. Aisopos continued his story.

"The Wolfman says, 'You rolled digamma again, so, you have a choice. Quit now, you can keep your house, land, and boy. Or, roll again. If you roll digamma, you keep all three, plus the Wolfman will give you a cow worth twenty-five drachma. But,'" Aisopos pointed his pointer finger, "'if you roll alpha to epsilon, the Wolfman takes it all. House, land, boy. You will never return to Attica again.'"

Aisopos's story was certainly making me feel like I was back in grade school, and I was becoming increasingly worried I would be asked to reiterate the moral by the end of it.

"My father, *putanas yos*. Two for two. He looked at me then, and I know what he was thinking. *Do I even care to win? Damp wood shack; loud, shit-dropping swans; rotten eggs; kid who never stops staring?* My father, *putanas yos*. He thinks, *I'll take my cow and buy myself a better life. Or, buy in for a higher bet.* So, the Wolfman came back the next day. But Aisopos, no." He pointed up at the same shelf, to a boat also whittled from wood, but painted with a coat of bright white. "I would be gone. I would already be at the port, so to sneak onto the boat to take me some place else. I slept in the tween deck. Got food from the scullery at night. They thought they only have a little rat. Me, Aisopos, a little rat. Then, after twenty-one days, the boat stopped."

Next to the boat was another old photograph, this one of a Japanese woman. Aisopos motioned for it. As I handed it to him, I read *1937* pencilled onto the back.

"I met my *glykó fasóli* in this new country. She had no home, no family. One day, we sneaked onto a train, and together, we came here." He pointed at the cabinet. The figurine next to the photo was a small piece of black steel.

"We worked at the factory. CCM, making bicycles, skates. We saved some money. Bought a little house. We lived in it, here, until my *glykó fasóli* died. At some point, Walmart came."

I couldn't believe what had just happened. Aisopos had spoken so much.

"You just happened to have all of these props to help tell your story?" I asked him.

"Yep," he said.

I scanned the cabinet. There were no other photos.

"Did you and *fasóli* have any children?"

"Nope."

I supposed, then, that Aisopos was now waiting for the reason as to why I was in his house that morning, sharing sandwiches, and admiring his cabinet of treasures. I pulled his chair back to its place at the other end of the sofa and handed him his didgeridoo. Then went over and picked up the die from the floor. I placed it back in its spot on the shelf and closed the glass panes.

Aisopos lifted himself out of his wheelchair and back onto the sofa. I sat in my seat across from him.

"You have a Neofinetia. An orchid. It's Japanese, but yours was from Walmart."

"One day I went to Walmart. I saw a flower there. The flower reminded me of my *glykó fasóli*. I bought it."

"That's it?"

"Yep."

"No other reason? No vigilante group affiliation, or connection to the fish that was left on your doorstep in the middle of January three and a half years ago?"

Aisopos blinked, as if he was beginning to not understand me.

"Have you ever had tapioca juice from the tapioca juice place on College Street?" I said.

He weaseled a handkerchief from the pocket of his sweatpants and blew his nose. Then picked up his sandwich from the sofa.

"Why is it that you keep Sarah as your tenant?" I said. "She's almost never steadily employed."

"Hey."

Sarah had returned, showered and dressed, and was now standing in the entrance of the living room. She was wearing a navy-blue pantsuit and her regularly fluffy brown hair that usually fell all over her face and shoulders had been neatly coiled into a tight knot at the top of her head. She had lipstick on. She looked like she was about to host a morning show. But also like she needed a few moments before going on air, because she was about to cry. Aisopos held out his handkerchief.

"I do my best," she said. "No thank you, Aisopos."

He shrugged and continued eating the sandwich, his focus back on the TV screen beside me. I didn't mean it like that. Like it was Sarah's fault. It wasn't.

"It's the world's fault," I said, but she just picked up my pillowcase from the floor and held it out to me.

"I'd give you your jacket, too, but you never took it off. Or your shoes."

She was right. There were many wet shoe prints all over Aisopos's yellowish-beige-ish carpet.

"Please don't cry," I said, taking the pillowcase.

"T-minus one minute," she said, ushering me up from the chair and over to the steps down to the front door. But I just couldn't be ushered yet. I knew if I looked back one more time, at that room Aisopos had spent like seventy years being inside of, I would see it, the flat-edged piece confirming his connection to BubbleHeaven2, whatever it was. Then I saw him glance back at the cabinet. So I did, too. Below the cupboards was a bottom shelf, and on that bottom shelf, next to a stack of ten-by-fourteen-by-four-inch parcels, approximately, was a second stack of small, ceramic bowls. I walked past Sarah, back across the living room, creating a new set of footprints across Aisopos's carpet.

"I have to go now, Austin," she said. "I have to get a job. Like you said."

I picked up one of the bowls and examined it.

"What does this say?" I asked Aisopos.

He looked at Sarah.

"He doesn't understand you," she said.

"Yes, he does," I said. "He's basically the narrator. Aisopos, what does this say? This writing on the side of the bowl?"

"He's tired now. Let him watch his shows."

"*Fasóli* must have taught you a little Japanese, no?"

Sarah walked over and took the bowl from my hand. "You're going to hurt his heart, Austin."

I took the paper from my pocket and pencil from my ear and crouched down at the coffee table.

"Place the bowl on the table, please. I need to copy it out."

She didn't. So I looked up at it in her hands, and copied it from there.

"What does this have to do with anything?" she said.

She needed to see the wall.

"Austin?" she said. "It's a bowl."

Aisopos banged the didgeridoo against the floor.

"Okay, finished. Thank you," I said to both Sarah and Aisopos, as I finally allowed myself to be ushered out of the house, because I knew he knew what I meant. He knew why I needed to see that bowl. He knew that Sarah was looking for a bedroom to rent after she'd graduated university and had to leave her student housing, and he knew that she would be helpful, that she would take on miscellaneous tasks as needed, such as tending to an orchid, and that she wouldn't be able to turn away a freezing fish. And he knew what was on its way to me next. But still, how had he signed up for Craigslist, let alone posted a rental ad for a bedroom, responded to a response, and arranged a contract for Sarah, all without the help of any children and their laptops, or Sarah, herself, with hers?

*

By the time I'd found myself in the laneway behind the old factory on that sunless morning, not for the first time wondering who that person was down there, closer to the door, wearing a safety vest and unloading something from the back of a van, I was no longer even convinced that Aisopos needed his wheelchair. As I got closer, I saw that the person had removed wooden stakes and a sign of some sort, and was carrying the stakes around to the front of the building. I went over to read the sign they'd leaned against the tire.

Notice, it read. *A change is proposed for this site. The city has received an application to change the Zoning Bylaw to allow the construction of a residential building.* The hammering out front echoed off the steel panels enveloping the building walls, causing some pigeons to fly up from a windowsill, beating their wings. Poop then plopped on the ground. What was going to happen next? A rusted bit of steel fell from a wall, landing on the asphalt with a tinny clang. It couldn't be this building for which the change was being proposed, could it? There were already residents residing within it. And while I only knew of two for certain, myself and Ronda, I certainly didn't think there were enough of us in total to warrant the creation of 109 parking spots plus 225 bike racks.

Once inside of my apartment, I dropped the pillowcase, opened the paper from my back pocket, then folded it so as to create a crease between *heavy chicken* and the writing I'd copied from the bowl. I tore the paper along the crease, then pinned the Japanese writing below the Japanese writing of Rock Party's note. As suspected, the first four characters were identical. So if Grear's translation was correct, the bowl read *tapioca*. What about the rest of Rock Party's note? The part she'd translated as "next life"? Could this be the life Aisopos's *glykó fasóli*, the original owner of the tapioca bowl, had departed to? Could tapioca even be slurped from a bowl?

I took a step back from the wall then, and another, so that I was standing in the centre of the room. Why was it that just as Aisopos and BubbleHeaven2 were coming together, the other stuff around me was about to be blown up and gutted and transformed in a way that would surely exploit the historic brickwork behind the stove? People lose their minds over bricks. Once they found out that Ronda and I were simply existing amongst them, there was no way they'd let us get away with staying for a quarter of the rent. They'd absolutely outbid us. Where was Ronda going to go then?

I picked the pillowcase up from the floor to get my phone and asked her: *where are you going to go?* The first answer that came up was a video for a song by Dave Matthews Band. I pressed play and watched as Dave walked, strumming his guitar, on a beach, in a desert, while somehow, simultaneously, watching an Adam Sandler and Winona Ryder film. In the sky? In his mind? I scrolled down to the next search result—a post from a forum that simply read, *Where are you going to go? I'm going to Bali.* I searched: *bali*. It seemed like a much better version of the place Dave Matthews was walking around in. More green. Misty. Quiet. It was also 15,839 kilometres away from Toronto.

I took two steps forward, dragged my fingernail over the guitar string between Rock Party's note and the origami cat. Then, from the Gardens to Aisopos. Dave Matthews was right when he claimed to have no reasons for us. Reasons being arguments as to why one should not leave. I couldn't blame Ronda for wanting to go to Bali, for wanting to get away from all of this. But what would I do without her? I followed the string from the origami cat to the ASMR Wikipedia page. Then back to the cat again. Back to Rock Party. I ran my fingernail over all six guitar strings, feeling six different vibrations, hearing six different pitches. Like six different voices, purring. I looked at my fingertip. It tingled.

"Wait, Ronda," I said, while typing *cat asmr good* into the search bar with my tingling fingertip. How had I not thought of this before? Video number one was of a cat in front of a microphone, eating kibble pieces that had been spread across a desk. When that ended, another video of three kittens bathing each other began, and played for almost fifteen minutes. Video number three was a cat batting at a dangling string. A small bell on its collar tinkled with each swipe.

I paused the video. Then went back to the start and replayed it. I knew that bell. I had seen that bell before, dangling from the base of a straw from which I'd sipped violet tapioca juice belonging to a young woman named Matilda, whose origami-enveloped phone number was now pinned to my wall. I searched: *cat asmr good japan* next. The first video listed featured a cat positioned like a sphinx on top of a table, appearing very content, while a young woman, face obscured by her hair, and wearing a bracelet of small glass beads, slowly ran a hand from the top of the cat's head all the way down its back. The cat kept its eyes closed, extending the fingers of its paws in an alternating pattern, until, eventually, it pushed itself up, and jumped out of frame. The video ended. I started it again. There was an orange cup with a square handle on the table. The table itself was like a thin tray, whitish-brownish in colour. A curtainless window behind it. The cat leapt. I paused the video. Started it again. The cat was orange and appeared to be in possession of all of its fur. The glass beads of the bracelet were clear and shaped like pebbles. After twelve strokes of the braceleted hand, a shadow filled the window, the cat stood, jumped. The video ended on the cup that remained undisturbed. I was watching the painting of Scoot. But that was not Scoot.

Who was in the window? I immediately messaged Tacka. And just as immediately, three dots appeared. Then disappeared. I looked up at the wall, at the emulation of the writing on Aisopos's bowl. The dots appeared again.

Sorry so.

You don't have to be sorry, I said. *I just want to know, who was in the video? In the window? And in the painting, too? Was it the same person?*

She didn't respond. I didn't blame her. I'd just sent five sentences all at once. I had so much to clarify, and, potentially, not enough time. I needed Tacka Attack Love to see the wall.

Tacka, video chat? ASMR?

OK.

Okay. But I'd need a computer first. And money.

Give me two hours, I said.

No, she said. *Later.*

Later than two hours?

What time?

Three dots.

Later, she said again.

Okay.

How many dollars? I said.

Yes, she said.

Yes, I repeated. *How many?*

But she'd stopped responding. If I wanted to know how much a private ASMR session with Tacka Attack Love was, I'd have to ask Hadir. It probably wouldn't be cheap, considering the half-million-dollar salary I'd discovered an ASMR specialist was capable of generating. It might even be as much, or more than I'd be able to get for the guitar. And I still needed to purchase bubble tea, and Sarah's latte, and a stay at the Holiday Inn, especially now that I was going to ask to borrow her laptop, on top of everything else.

I messaged Hadir.

How much does it cost for an ASMR session with Tacka?

A moment later, he replied, *Who?*

Oh my god, Hadir.

Ohhhh. DOTA babe. 50 bucks, 15 mins.

"Ronda," I said, as I began to type, *How can I make fifty dollars before later in Japan?*

The first suggestion Ronda made was that I sign up to be a Lyft driver, which would have been a good idea, considering the weather, but was no longer possible since I'd already sold the car. Her second suggestion—to sign up for Instant Approval Credit Card with a Zero Rejections Policy—was, however, not only possible, but was an even more logical suggestion than the third, which was to sell unused items I had around my home, because all I had to do was input my name, birthday, address, annual salary, social insurance number, then tap the word *Agree*. I could then begin to use the number associated with my new credit card immediately, just as the two smiling young men on the front page of the website were, while holding hands in a bakery, purchasing cookies, with but a simple tap of my cell phone. With this credit card, not only would I be able to pay Tacka Attack Love, but I could also purchase the strings I needed to up the value of my guitar prior to selling it, and treat Sarah to a professionally baked cookie on her first day at whatever new job she was going to end up in. I messaged Hadir:

Does she accept credit?
Who the hell gave you a credit card?
How do you pay her?
Like paypal, he said.

And to use PayPal, I'd need the credit card. So it seemed, then, that every problem was pointing to one solution. Within five minutes, I'd signed up, acquired $2,500, and was purchasing a new set of guitar strings from Cosmo Music—The Musical Instrument Superstore! Once I'd agreed to all of PayPal's fine print, I was well on my way to later in Japan.

Finally, I sent a message to Sarah.

Could I borrow your computer tonight?

While I waited for her response, I turned my attention back to the wall, to the bottom of it, this time, where it met the box of fax paper pushed up against it. I crouched down and separated a sheet, took the pencil from my ear, and drew a rectangle. In the centre of the rectangle, I wrote, *Who?* Then I stood and tacked the window in question to the wall.

CHAPTER 8

No More Coincidences

I cannot say I believe in coincidences. Not anymore. To believe it was a coincidence that Brad and Kirk showed up in the laneway behind the old factory after Hadir had not only called me following our conversation over text message, but shared his belief that I was following a pattern of cock-induced self-destructive behaviour because of this so-called obsession I had with the "DOTA babe," even though he could tell she was a very beautiful woman, an eight or a nine, in his words, because of her voice, which was like that of a geisha's, but that the combination of uncharacteristic probing plus lurking behaviours I'd recently begun displaying were becoming troubling to an unsuitable degree, even by his own generally cock-motivated standards, and to not say something about it now, before things reached a potentially *Dateline* level of sketchiness, would be just plain unconscionable.

"Let me be as clear as possible about the partially completed framework of the puzzle tacked to the wall in front of me," I had told Hadir in response. "This miscellany is in no way indicative of a threat to the safety of Tacka Attack Love, or anyone else, for that matter. In fact, the real concern here is the closed-up tofu shop in Taitō Ward upon which BadDog has crafted his psychotic mural, and the eerie look-a-like paintings he is possibly creating based upon YouTube videos featuring animals that he likely wants to eat. I am trying to help Tacka Attack Love, and Rock Party, and Matilda, by figuring out who, in Canada, is aligned with, or even working for, BadDog, or who, as the case may be, could be held responsible for the appearance of Scoot, and framing of me for his murder. In fact, while I have you on the phone, tell me, Hadir, have you ever experienced another form of ASMR via DOTA, particularly that which would be created by the sounds of a cat in some way?"

To which Hadir responded by calling me a crackbrain and a fruit, and told me he was cutting me out of his life forever because of the risk I imposed on his own mental health. I told him, "You do this. I've already cut you out of my life, and now you are displacing your own feelings of inferiority and shame onto me by way of accusing me of taking drugs. For some reason, it always seems as though you want to hold me back, Hadir. It seems like you do not want me to move forward in my life any more than you can move in yours."

So when I received the call from Brad telling me to come downstairs, and that he had McDonald's, the first thing I told him was that I was not stupid, I could not be bribed, and I was not in the mood for a burger anyway, as I'd had enough instant ramen and was fine. The second thing I told him was that anything Hadir had said about *Dateline* was based on his lack of clarity concerning the significance of very select articles of information, of which he might actually be more privy to than he's letting on, because if Hadir had proven anything over the course of our relationship as so-called friends who supposedly related more like so-called brothers, it was that he liked to feel important, but he could not be trusted with any actual important things.

Of course, Brad's response, being that he apparently had no idea what I was talking about, was expected, but the real giveaway was the sound of Kirk, who was complaining loudly about the retard who'd forgotten his spicy buffalo sauce. Kirk, whose presence, up until that moment, I was unaware of, was what indicated that there definitely was, without a doubt, something going on beyond the invitation to eat fast food in an alley.

"Kirk is here?" I said to Brad.

"We met up before then came over together. Chill."

"You've never done that before. Ever. You have never met up with Kirk and then come together as a couple to see me at my house."

"You don't live in a house."

"What do you want?"

"Come the fuck outside," Kirk yelled. What a goon. Seriously. I couldn't stand that guy. Plus, this was not his idea. All Kirk ever did was sit back and wait for everyone else to do everything around him. Clean out stuff. Take stuff to the Goodwill. Take stuff to the dump. Whatever. I hung up, then went down to the elevator and out the back door. Brad was standing by the wall all stiff and cold-looking with his peacoat unbuttoned, holding a McDonald's bag from which Kirk was pulling out fries like ten at a time and shoving them down his own throat.

"See? I have not self-destructed," I said.

"All I see is a guy who says he doesn't do crack looking like a guy who does crack," said Kirk, spitting fry chunks.

"Fuck you," I said.

He whipped a fry at me.

"Go ahead," he yelled. "Come at me, crackhead."

"You're selling all your stuff," said Brad. "That's suicide-y and drug-doer-like."

"Would a suicidal drug-doer have over two thousand dollars in available credit?" I said.

"I don't know, possibly," he replied.

"I've never done drugs," I shouted. "You guys do drugs. You guys go to bars and drink and do coke. Hadir was trying to sabotage me, as per usual."

"Where are you going to live when they finally blow up this crack den?" said Kirk.

"I'll figure that out after."

"After what? Some of the windows are already boarded up."

"After I video chat with Tacka and figure out who the passing form in the window was. Why Aisopos's late wife had a tapioca bowl, and why Matilda gave me her phone number. Why Rock Party has the painting acquired by Her from BadDog, the results of the art contest, and who, amongst all of these people, has been to Missouri. Let me figure that stuff out first, and then I'll figure out where to live. Okay? Now, for all I know, Ronda could be boarding a flight out of Canada at any moment. I can't talk to Tacka at the library, because I need to show her the wall, so Sarah's going to bring her computer over. I think. She hasn't answered me yet."

"Let's go," Kirk said to Brad.

"Thank you," I said.

"You need to get a job, and you need to get the car back," Brad said. From some distance away, sirens were approaching.

"Take the subway," I said, turning my back to them to lift the bolt. I stuck the key in the padlock. And then it happened.

"What just happened?" said Brad.

"There's no point in you waiting around to see what I do next," I said.

"Did your key just break?"

It had.

"No," I said.

"It wasn't Hadir," Kirk said.

I closed my fist over the half-broken key and turned to face them.

"Dan doesn't know what he's talking about, either. He has an anger problem, and most of what he says is his problem talking."

Brad laughed.

"It wasn't Dan either, buddy," said Kirk. "You know Sarah's in freaking love with you, right? For some reason. Who the fuck knows. But seriously, she's probably your only shot at ever having a semi-normal girlfriend."

"Sarah is a whole-normal person. She's the most level-headed human that exists in this entire world right now."

"Okay," he yelled back, as he'd already started walking down the laneway without even checking to see if Brad was following him. "Whatever you say, crackhead."

The sirens were passing then. A fleet, it sounded like. Brad said something else to me, but I didn't hear any of it because of them, so I shook my head no since there wasn't anything he could have said that I would have responded to affirmatively. Then he started walking away, too. Kirk had already disappeared. I couldn't tell you if Brad ever caught up to him, if he even wanted to, or what they needed the car for. I can tell you, though, that if there was any food in that bag for me, they were both happy I didn't actually eat it.

*

Out front of Grear's, the person in the silver bodysuit was now shooting two tandem yo-yos from their fingertips while posing like Spider-Man.

"Shop's closed," they said.

"What did you need to purchase?" I asked them.

"Fuse."

They lived in a place with electricity?

"Why are you doing that?" I said, regarding the yo-yos, and poses.

"Coordination. Reflexes like a star-nosed mole."

Kirk could be a person like this. A person who tries to convince the public that they were simply blowing fuses and going to stores, while on the inside, they were actually thinking about something as frightening as the reaction times of small mammals. That wouldn't surprise me.

"Sink trap, too," the person said. "You know when the sink spits all the food back out?" They shot a yo-yo in my direction. "I need a sink trap, too."

Where was Grear, anyway? Why was she closed? She hadn't been closed in probably a year. Did the impending development scheme encompass the row of shops next to the former factory I currently lived in, which included hers, as well? Was she already on her way to some place more lush and restorative? I didn't think Grear was the type to go to a place like Bali, but then, all of the grey, up and down, everywhere you looked in this place—over time, I supposed, it could change a person.

I'd found myself walking toward the park then, to the place where the garbage I didn't pick up was still blocking the path. Less brown now, and more black, like it was all so frostbitten by this point that it was practically dead. It was a pile of dead garbage around which people had since created a side trail in the snow.

In fact, two people were walking on that trail just as I was approaching it, and weren't even observing the ground, or the change in their route as it was happening. Simply, reflexively, not seeing. *Don't you see that?* I would have asked them, if they weren't already having a loud and frankly accusatorial conversation between themselves about one or the other having sex with someone they shouldn't have had sex with. But I did ask it to the person who came next. He took out one earbud and looked at the ground, and then at me, and then kept walking. He really didn't see it.

So, was it there, or not? This question seemed to be all around me, in the form of golden lights, wreaths, garlands, bows, bells and fir trees in front of expensive camping gear stores, as I kept on walking. If all of this stuff really existed, why did everyone look so serious? Why were they all dressed in austere black coats like Brad's? With their buttons undone? It was cold. It was snowing and raining at the same time, yet there were people riding bicycles through traffic as if it weren't. How was it that no one seemed disrupted by the never-ending sequence of sirens passing in all directions, at every block? They all just talked louder, or else were wearing their earbuds, and staring. And the further I went, the darker it became. The buildings became taller. If you looked to the windows above, the glass only seemed to reflect back black coats. If you weren't wearing one, like I was not, it would appear to be that, at least within the business district of Toronto, you were but a mirage.

Where were we, the less well-dressed corporeal? I didn't know. There was a time when I would have answered, *Hadir's neighbourhood. There is a substantial spectrum of quality and colour in the clothing and outerwear there.* But I wasn't even sure about that anymore. It had been a long time since I'd actually gone there to walk around and eat Bangladeshi food and soft serve with Hadir or his dad.

Or his mom. For all I knew, the new developments, and the funereal apparel they brought along with them, were moving in there, too.

When I reached the docks, where it was rainier and snowier, as well as windier, I couldn't help but think that this might be the place. The place where there was currently nobody, except a person who worked at the gate, and myself. If the pirate ship here ever left the lake, I might have simply sneaked on deck, down the hatch to the hold, and went where it went; slept up in the longboat some nights, stole food from the galley, sailed south until we crossed the Panama Canal to Peru, where I'd hop a bus to Bolivia, make a home in an altitude too high to breathe in and raise many heavy chickens.

The person who worked at the gate locked it and left. Was I the only one who saw them, too? Was I the only one who could see this place at all, once no one was here working anymore? Those approaching from the street simply circumnavigated it, or turned around completely to backtrack from their approach, like the pet section at Walmart—was I the only person who could see that place? Was I the only person who could see Scoot?

No. Because Sarah. Sarah saw everything. And if she were there with me, she would have seen it all: water, pirate ship, avoidant people. Why was she trying to look away now? I felt my pocket for my phone to call her, but it wasn't there. It was over an hour away on foot, on the other side of the city, in the former factory that was my home, which I was locked out of, and that would soon be demolished from the inside out. Instead, I took out the half key. Its edge was jagged. Not enough to cut my thumb, but if I pressed it against my leg, it could have gone in. In an unexpected turn of events, I could have found myself in the emergency room with half of a key stuck in my thigh. *Can you take this out, please?* I would have asked the nurses at triage. *And when you're finished, please, could you give it back to me? I'd like to loop a string through the ring hole, tie the ends of that string together, then adorn the lid of a reusable tapioca cup with it.* I would have liked to have sent the message to all the animalists out there watching that I, Austin, was not afraid of a puncture wound.

But who was I kidding? I didn't have a reusable tapioca cup. While I did have the credit to purchase one, I didn't have access to my phone to do so. What's more, where would I have purchased the string? With Grear's closed, I put the broken key back into my pocket and left that place, visible or not, the way I'd arrived at it: by walking for a long time up many streets that glittered, or did not, where passersby passed me, or through me, in rain and snow that was or was not falling, until I was outside of the Bubble Heaven on College Street, and it was dark, and I was looking in through the window at the multi-chromatic party that had already begun while a mist of grape-scented vapour obscured my view.

"Matilda," I called, knocking on the window.

A girl in an army green trench coat and a black toque that distended upward as if to cover a second head on top of her first broke out of the huddle. "You looking for Matilda?" she said.

"Yes."

"She has a performance, man. Won't be done till ten. No use yelling like that."

She was holding green juice in a clear plastic cup—green like the flavour of which Tacka was potentially fond.

"Can I try that?" I asked her.

"My drink?"

"Yes."

"No. What the fuck?"

"Do you know what time it is right now?" I asked any of the vapers, really, but the army girl was the only one to answer. Without not looking at me, she pulled her phone from the inside pocket of her coat.

"Why you looking for Matilda?" she asked.

I pointed to her cup. "Hers has a bell," I said.

She checked her phone.

"It's 9:30," she said.

"Do you know where her performance is?"

"You joking?"

Why would I be joking?

"I don't know, man, I see her walking around the park near Trinity sometimes. But whatever it is you're looking for, I don't think she's got it. Matilda's a good girl."

Matilda's a good girl?

"I, myself, however, can probably swing a deal. How much do you have?"

I didn't understand basically anything this person was talking about, and our conversation was really cutting into the small window of time I had to try and catch Matilda passing through the park near Trinity after her performance. How much of what? I had one pair each of socks and shoes, pants, a shirt and a jacket on me. Most of those things were wet.

"Other than what you see, I have this," I told her, presenting the half key from my pocket. "I might need it, though. You can't keep it."

She looked at my hand, then sipped her drink. "Matilda's got some fucked-up secret life going on, don't she?"

"I believe so," I said, and carried onward.

*

In the dark, standing next to a large tree trunk, it was hard to detect distinctions amongst the spattering of heads moving about, but soon enough, in and amongst a small crowd that had just exited a building across the street, there appeared one with a very straight line of hair cut to her chin. The group slowly broke apart as each person walked off in a different direction, but Matilda walked closer and closer toward me. When she was about a foot away, I moved outward from the tree. She screamed.

"How was your performance?" I asked her.

"You?" she yelled. "What are you doing here?"

"Catching you."

She looked around. To check if there were people in witnessing-distance, I supposed.

"Are you stalking me?" she said.

"I understand it might be startling to suddenly see a person you weren't expecting to see."

"At night, in a park."

"I can assure you, I have never in my life stalked anyone, including you. I have, however, been thinking of you. May I walk with you a bit?"

"Why didn't you call me first?"

"My phone, at this point, is about thirty minutes away by foot. So, may I?"

After a moment, Matilda agreed. I would have also guessed that she appeared to have a slight smile on her face, though her hair had fallen a little ways in front of it, and gotten stuck there, upon her lips, once again. So I couldn't be sure.

"Perhaps you've been thinking of me, as well," I said.

"I have to get back to my residence. I have a bus first thing in the morning."

"Headed where?"

"My parents.'"

"What sort of performance were you performing in, anyway?"

"Choir. Carols."

Matilda sure had a lot going on.

"Plus, it's shitty out," she said. "It's like, raining and snowing at the same time."

It was true. It was time to move things forward.

"Other than studying, singing and attending to your family, what else do you do with your spare time?"

"I volunteer sometimes. With seniors. I go to their homes and do small tasks, or just sit and talk with them."

Aisopos was a senior.

"You have a bell on a string looped around the base of your straw where it connects to the lid of your personal tapioca juice cup," I said. "From where did you acquire this bell, and for what reason did you choose to accessorize your cup with it?"

If she wasn't before, she was definitely smiling now. Also, maintaining quite widely opened eyes. "More like, why did you even notice that?" she asked me.

"Tapioca juice is a new juice to me. These accessorized cups are new cups to me."

"They sell them at the store. And online, too."

"But, why a bell of the sort which you would attach to a cat collar?"

"I found it and thought it was cute."

"Where did you find it?"

"By the water one day."

"The water I was just near?"

We stopped at the edge of the park, across from which was a building where Matilda claimed to maintain residency. She stood in front of me.

"Which water were you just near?"

"The one near the docks downtown."

"Yeah, that water. You know, you choose strange topics to talk about."

What was strange were the circumstances under which I'd met Matilda. This had nothing to do with me as a person who asks questions of other people. By the way, how did she learn the ancient Japanese art of paper folding, and why, of all the possible shapes she could have folded, did she choose to utilize such skills in order to create a cat out of her phone number?

"Do you ever help seniors write Craigslist ads for prospective renters?"

"Actually, yes."

"Do you like animals?" I asked her.

"What?"

"I mean, do you like animals in the sense that you want to save them from harm?"

"Well, of course," she said. "If I were in any situation where I could keep a living creature safe from harm, of course I would do whatever I had to. Why are you asking me this?"

"What about YouTube? Have you seen the ASMR video with the cat and the bell?"

"I mean, I'd invite you in to watch stuff, but like I said, I've got a bus in the morning. We could meet again? After the holidays?" She placed her hand on my arm near my shoulder. "You can ask me any weird questions you want then."

"If I have more questions," I said.

She removed her hand, giving my arm a little tap as she did so. I wasn't sure what that meant. I wasn't sure when after the holidays was, either, but in the end, that was where I left things with Matilda; her crossing a street and entering a well-lit and heated building, me continuing to walk, wondering what the odds were that Matilda had been the one to help Aisopos find Sarah. Like I said, I could no longer believe in coincidences. To accept it was simply a coincidence that Matilda would also find, of all things, a bell of the sort that would be attached to the collar of a cat near the docks where I had only just found myself a short period of time ago pre-finding her for a second time would be preposterous.

At this point, I could only assume that Matilda had, at some point, seen, received, or in some other way been made aware of a message—potentially threatening and possibly in the form of an animal, perhaps even the animal I had received, from BadDog, his international cronies, or the gang of animalist pirates hunting for his reward—then had quite purposefully chosen to sit in the booth (in which I had been sitting twenty-four hours ago) in order to tell me about said awareness (indirectly, by way of displaying her bell), having previously known that I would eventually end up at the tapioca restaurant, from where, afterward, I would go on to witness the third YouTube video of the jingling bell attached to the cat batting the string, because of her conceivable prior knowledge of Aisopos, his dead *glykó fasóli*, Tacka Attack Love, and even, for all I knew, Rock Party.

At present, however, I needed to turn my attention away from Matilda and toward the act of seeking shelter, and the overhang above the entrance to the library closest to the former factory and present condominium development where I was locked out of was the first spot large enough to cover my body that I'd come to, so long as I kept my legs parallel to the door. This was not suicide-y or drug-doer-like. This was not self-destruction. This was just where the Birdman, stalking past on the street that night, found me.

He stopped on the sidewalk at the end of the ramp. I didn't move, hoping I was enshrouded in enough darkness that he wouldn't notice me there. But he turned his whole self to face me. It appeared he had either a very long and protrusive nose, or a beak, possibly of the papier mâché sort, strapped over his ears. After a moment, he took one stilted step forward. Another. Then, quickly, he stilted right up the ramp and stood over top of me.

"Don't," I said.

"Don't what?"

At first, I couldn't answer. Then he made a pecking motion with his head.

"That," I said.

"This?" he said, raising his wings, which I could see then were made of garbage bags and shredded scarves.

"Or that."

"This will be mine," he said.

"What will?"

He fanned a wing in a semi-circle.

"The entranceway to the library?" I said.

He stomped a stilt. "Move," he shouted.

"Why are you doing this? Why did BadDog do this?"

He stomped the other stilt, this time much closer to my foot.

"Caw," he screamed.

I had two options then. Sprint, or kick a stilt out from beneath him. Or, potentially, I could gamble my way out of this situation.

"There doesn't happen to be a die in one of those bags on your arms, does there?"

But he'd already started barricading me by way of hopping back and forth between his two stilts, all while doing that horrifying head thing. I shimmied up from the ground with my back against the door, waiting for an Austin-sized gap in his movement.

"You need to let me sprint away," I tried to tell him, but he just kept saying "Caw," as if I would know what that meant. "I'm just going to go now, then," I shouted. "Don't say I didn't warn you."

I ducked and covered my head with one arm while sticking the other straight out like a sword, stabbing the Birdman in the thigh, at first, and then in the wing, a bag of which tore off and clung to my fingertips as I kept sprinting, down the ramp, up the sidewalk, through sleet, through an intersection, even though sirens were approaching, past the hardware store, and into the front of a car turning out of the laneway. The driver honked. I stood there for a moment, feeling the hood through the gross garbage bag. Then I squeezed around the side of the car and kept sprinting toward a dumpster in a parking spot beside the former factory, where I stopped, momentarily, to shake the bag off me. Freed, I lowered my sword and went over to the bolted and padlocked steel door of my soon-to-not-be home.

If Scoot could find a way in, so could I.

CHAPTER 9

Jagged Edges

If I were a Scoot, I thought, *I'd probably start by circling the perimeter of the building, searching for a hole at ground level big enough to squeeze my body through, either by way of sniffing for a change in temperature, or by keeping close enough to the wall so as to be able to feel for a gap with either my whiskers or body.* The thing about these walls, though, was that although they were, in fact, very riddled with holes, as far as I could tell they'd all been patched in one way or another, either with concrete, bricks or boards of wood. There were plenty of dents in the steel siding, too, but no actual fractures. If any existed in the foundation of the building, they probably began elsewhere, created by animals much smaller than myself, such as a mouse, or vole, which tunnelled underground, and led not directly to the interior but to the space between the earth and the interior, where things like pipes existed. If I couldn't fit in one of these holes as a cat, there was certainly no chance I could fit in one as a man.

So in this situation, then, I supposed I'd need to resort to jumping, so as to get to the next level of the building where there were windows with potential holes, such as Austin's, although his was another storey up from the second, so jumping to that specific window was, as of yet, out of the question. The first set of windows were high enough that I would require a certain degree of boosting—the height of a dumpster, if pushed closer to the building. Or a van, parked at a weird angle on a sidewalk next to one side of the building, with one corner of the rear close enough to the wall, so that if a cat were to jump onto the hood and then, subsequently, the roof of the vehicle, it could potentially jump to the ledge of the window above. Did that windowpane have a hole in it? I couldn't tell. It was dark. And, of course, neither would Scoot. Be able to tell. Because he was blind.

So, I climbed onto the hood. Then, subsequently, the roof of the vehicle. Using a dent as a foothold, I pulled myself up the wall to bring my knees onto the sill, then shifted onto the balls of my feet, being, then, in some sort of squatted, gargoyle-like position, and pushed against the panes to see if they would budge. They wouldn't. A man crossed the street and approached the van. I stayed as still as possible. He was looking down at a phone in his hand. Even as he took his keys from his coat pocket and unlocked the door, and even still as he opened the door and sat down inside the van, he was looking at his phone. What could have possibly had him so enraptured? YouTube? Would he have noticed if I were to climb back down onto the roof of his vehicle at that point? He hadn't even closed his door. Then suddenly, he started yelling and cursing. What could have happened on YouTube to make him so upset? Why had he even parked here in the first place, instead of in a parking lot? It certainly wasn't legal. Was he a criminal? He was definitely a loose cannon. If he caught me climbing back onto his vehicle, who knows what he might do. I didn't. What I did know, though, once he finally pulled his door shut and sped over the sidewalk to get onto the road, was that I was now stuck up on a window ledge with only two options to get unstuck: climbing higher or falling down.

    I looked higher, up a telephone pole beside the window to its first set of wires, along those wires, and to the corner of a billboard in front of the wall of the building adjacent to the wall I was currently on. If I fell, I'd likely injure a body part. I could then go to the hospital, where I'd predictably be able to rest in an emergency room chair for a while, and then some more in a bed for a while, presumably until an hour in the morning that wouldn't be long from the time at which Grear would potentially return and open her shop, if she hadn't already left the country. However, all of those hours spent resting in a hospital were hours Tacka could potentially be messaging my phone, still inside my apartment, to tell me that it was now later in Japan. If I were a Scoot, I would, in all likelihood, scoot along the edge of the ledge, and, hoping there would be a billboard with a catwalk to land upon, jump again.

    Gripping the wall with my fingertips, I stood up on the ledge and aligned my feet so they were pointing in the direction of the billboard, and jumped. I caught the edge of the catwalk on the back of the billboard, and pulled myself up onto it, and from there I could see that the window next to the window directly behind the billboard had a hole in the pane that had been stuffed with a pillow. The pillow from the bed upon which I, Scoot, would so much like to perch, if I were alive, and which also I, Austin, could possibly reach from the other corner of the catwalk. With my palms pressed against the sign, I sidestepped my way over to that corner, then turned around to face the window. I fit a foot into another foothold dent, so that I was balanced between the wall and the sign, then reached for the pillow, and pulled. As it tore open, bits of white fabric and fluff all gently floated to the dark ground, like I, some kind of prop master suspended over the set of a music video, was making it snow more beautiful snow than actual snow ever actually was.

I climbed over to the ledge of the window behind the billboard, scooted to its edge, and stepped over to the ledge of my window, used the remainder of the pillow like a boxing glove, and punched out the bits of glass that were still attached to the window frame. Then went in feet first, into the kitchenette sink, where glass crunched beneath my shoes.

The phone, on the floor, was a mere percentage point away from death. There were no missed calls from Sarah, no messages from Tacka. I connected the phone to Dan's charger, which itself was connected to the electrical outlet behind the nightstand, which, prior to the purchasing and hiding of the cat treats from Missouri, had powered the lamp still on the floor, and sat down beside it to wait. The weather outside was coming inside. First, in weird yowls through the hole, second, in sporadic splatters against the countertops. Third, in a cold that crept along the walls of the apartment, which, to be honest, was beginning to feel less like an apartment, or even a former office, and more like a very dark trap three storeys high in the sky, with no easy way in or out.

The last normal time Sarah came over, I can recall there being light around us, regardless of the lamp being unplugged. The light was yellow. It could have been from the moon, or even the stars, through the window above the sink. It could have been a refraction from a phone screen tilted upward that was mirroring the corn sweater Scoot was curled upon, or the body of the guitar. The memory of that space did not match the space I was currently inside of. Why? Perhaps because of the sky that was black most hours of the day and night. Or, the sky that was grey during the few hours in between the black sky. Or, the red on the phone screen from blood I didn't realize was escaping my body somehow.

    I scanned myself. Both the sleeve of my coat and the now-exposed tricep beneath it had a vertical slice running through them. I got up from the floor and went over to the kitchenette where, still stuck in the window frame, a piece of broken glass was flecked with frosting blood. There was blood on the countertop and in the sink, and blood shoeprints on the floor, where there were also more glass shards. Snow had absorbed some of it, but then the snow had melted, thus carrying it through the kitchenette in little blood rivers. What was I supposed to do? I didn't have any paper towels to dab it all up. I didn't have a dustpan to sweep the glass into, or a broom with which to even sweep. I had nothing, anymore, anywhere, it seemed, in a place where I'd almost had it all.

    With each step backward, I shook my shoes, so as to track as little glass as possible any farther inside. I walked backward until my back was to the wall, at the bottom of which was the pillowcase. I picked it up and wrapped it around my coat sleeve and arm until the slices were covered, then held it in place while I pulled the lace from one of my shoes. That's when I realized I was wearing two shoes, and thus, had a second lace that, if needed, could be used as either a clue, or a charm string. Holding one end of the first lace with my teeth, I wrapped it around the pillowcase, then tied the two ends into a knot. Next, using the hockey stick, I went back to the kitchenette, picked up the largest piece of glass from the floor, then Michigan-ed it right out the window. Once I'd shot all the glass I possibly could with a hockey stick, I tossed it onto the bed and sat back down on the floor beside the phone, the face of which I then wiped clean against my pants. Still no message from

Tacka. How long would I be waiting? How many haircuts could she possibly be going to?

*

At 3:23 am, I woke up.

You have in DOTA? Tacka asked.

No, I don't.

OK.

A circle then appeared on my phone screen with Tacka Attack Love's display picture inside of it. I was being invited to join her, it said. I accepted. The screen went dark. There was some shuffling, breathing, then a flash of light that shrunk back to a glowing orb in the top left corner of the screen. I could see Tacka's hair shining below it. The rest was shadows. She started making plopping noises. Like a leaking tap. Or was that my tap?

"Tacka?" I said. "Is that you making that sound?"

"What you can like?"

What I can like?

"What I do like?" I said.

"This?"

More plopping noises.

"Tacka, I can't really see you. It's very dark."

As I spoke, I noticed movement on the bottom half of the screen. I snapped my fingers and the sound boomeranged through the phone.

"I think that's me down there," I said. "I can't really see me, either."

Tacka snapped her fingers.

"I was just testing," I told her. But she did it again. Consistently, like she was making some kind of beat. Then started whispering "dark," repeating the *k* sound until she'd run out of breath and had to start over. A gentle tickle ran along my scalp. But I wasn't tickling myself. Was it the wind? I looked over the bed to the hole above the sink. Is wind a thing you can see?

"Dark," Tacka continued to aspirate, then stopped snapping, and began to rub her palms together, it sounded like. Somewhere beyond the veil of darkness, she must have been very near to a microphone, because the sound coming through my own phone sounded more like a shower streaming soft, hot water from a very stainless steel, rectangular shower head, within a glass-doored, grey-and-white-tiled shower stall that had recently been Tilex-ed. I closed my eyes. I saw Sarah, her rainbow mittens cupping the backs of my hands, eyebrows fluffed in a frown of concern as she breathed warm air onto my cold, damp fingers. I could have stood there forever with her, wasting water and credit. Until she looked up at me, Matilda, head tilted, blunt hairline brushing against her shoulder. Yet another piece of it stuck to her lip. She pulled off a mitten with her teeth and spat it on the ground, then ran her fingertip slowly up my forearm to my inner elbow.

"Stop," I yelled.

The phone was quiet. Dark and quiet.

"Tacka, I need to show you something," I said. "I believe you have information, very particular information, that I, Austin, particularly need. But it's impossible for us to understand each other without some kind of cryptograph. So I just need to show you."

"Stop?" she said.

"Stop this. Whatever this is. The ASMR."

"Stop," she whispered, repeating the *p*. She blew gently into her microphone. I reached between the bed and the nightstand and unplugged Dan's phone charger, then crawled to the other side of the nightstand and took up the lamp, pinching my way along its cord until I found the end of it, in the dark, which I then plugged into the outlet from where I'd unplugged the phone charger. Then I stood up, put the lamp back up on the nightstand, and turned the phone to face the wall. "Look," I said. "You can't see it all at once in a tiny rectangle like this, but Sarah's computer isn't here, so it will have to do."

Tacka was quiet. I turned the phone back to check if she was still there. Her hair twinkled. I moved closer to the wall.

"This is the Wikipedia entry on ASMR. While I'm aware information shared on Wikipedia is not always one hundred percent reliable, I assume what's been included here provides an accurate enough understanding of the experience, although it is notably missing the general ASMR technician's pay rate. I had to Google that after. This paper represents you."

Still, quiet.

"This cat, which is also, technically, a piece of paper, represents my new acquaintance, Matilda, who, as you can see, is connected to both you and this note I've copied from the thirty-third photo posted to Rock Party's Instagram account, because all three of you are in possession of a charm looped around the base of the straws attached to your own personal tapioca juice cups, and which may, or may not, indicate your allegiance to a movement intending to take down a different movement of animalists, who not only brought a cat to the location where I'm currently residing, but also potentially a fish to the location where my friend, at least she was at that moment in time, Sarah, was residing, which is the home of the person signified by this paper, upon which has been written his name: Aisopos. Aisopos has a Neofinetia, an orchid of the same species which you have featured as the most recent photo on your own Instagram account, as well as those currently being displayed at the Missouri Botanical Gardens.

"All of this is to say that, somehow, the subject of the painting which your sister, Her, had given you, which you then gave to Rock Party, and then subsequently photographed, was a cat whom I believe a sinister muralist from Tokyo is offering a large sum of much reward for, and this muralist is also currently at risk of having more of their work displayed at a café and art gallery in Setagaya City, thereby instilling more fear into the public consciousness by way of winning a contest. But that's getting ahead. I named the cat Scoot and very recently, I had to pretend to be him in order to break into my own apartment. It worked, and now I'm talking to you. So, do you know this artist, BadDog? And is that him, looking in the window, in both the painting, and in the live-action version of the painting, *cat asmr good japan*, on YouTube?"

All Tacka Attack Love replied with was her breath. I turned the phone back around to face my face, which was visible now, albeit through what looked like a layer of lint.

"You like laundry?" she said.

"Laundry?"

"You say, you like laundry."

We were both quiet for a moment then. Did she truly have nothing to say about any of the information I'd just shown her?

"Tacka," I said. "Did you make the video on YouTube where the cat jumps off the table?"

Nothing. There was no way of knowing which words she understood when I spoke, or what groups of words she herself was, or was not, willing to speak aloud in English. Was it possible there was information she was literally able to tell me, but figuratively could not? Was the truth even there, somewhere, buried in the Instagram account of Tacka Attack Love?

"I have no laundry soap," I said.

She appeared to nod her shining head.

"To Tenchi I have cat."

Pardon?

"At hospital so."

"What is Tenchi?" I said.

"Rock Party."

Rock Party's name is Tenchi?

"You have a cat with Rock Party?"

"Yes."

"But by have, you mean do?"

Silence. What does Tacka do?

"ASMR," I said.

"Yes," said Tacka.

"You have cat ASMR with Rock Party at the hospital?"

"Yes."

"Is the cat at the hospital right now?"

"Hospital Fukuoka."

"But, now?"

Nothing. Tacka didn't know the word *now*.

"Presently?" I said.

"Have hospital tomorrow," she said.

"You're going to the hospital tomorrow?"

"Yes."

"Okay, but what about the video? Was the video created at the hospital?"

She didn't answer. I looked up at the wall, at the window I'd drawn with the word *Who?* in the centre. Who would be passing by the window of a hospital? And to which wall, of which wing, did this window belong? Some place where an animal is allowed, regardless of the sanitary issues involved. What ailments or illnesses were not so serious that proper sanitary measures couldn't be relaxed a little?

"Austin?" said Tacka.

I held up the phone I'd let drop in my hand.

"Austin, bye," she said. Then the circle with Tacka's picture in it appeared again, as well as the time code, *15:00*.

I logged onto PayPal and tapped the option to send money to Tacka Attack Love. Was it possible Rock Party had been at the hospital this entire time? Since the foremost moment from whence I sent Tacka my first message? For the duration of the entire contest at Hōnto No Kimochi Gallery and Café? Why were they even at the hospital? What happened? Why did the cat in the video look like Scoot, but without all the eyes and portions of paws and fur missing? I reopened Instagram and searched for Rock Party, tapping on the most recent photo posted, posted not exactly recently, but nearly six and a half weeks ago on November 10. Was that the last photo taken of Rock Party before going to the hospital? I felt for the pencil behind my ear so I could write this date onto the calendar. But the pencil wasn't there. I went back over to the edge of the kitchenette to check if it was in the sink. It wasn't. It wasn't on the floor, either. Had it fallen in the process of my breaking into my own apartment?

I opened a new page on my phone and searched for the YouTube video of the jumping cat. If I was correct in my interpretation of Tacka Attack's mistranslation of the word *have*, and the cat was at the hospital with Rock Party, then the date the video was uploaded must have fallen after the date of the final posted photo. But it didn't. The video was created on September 20, fifty-two days prior to Rock Party's potential hospital admission. So, what came first? The video, or the intake date? Was there a back and forth going on? An in and out? A timeline running only as smooth as the jagged edge of a window frame after the glass of the window was punched through it? It would seem that way, especially for Tacka, whose comings and goings were about as abrupt as a point on a piece of said broken glass. As well as for the cat, being on a table one moment, then jumping off it the next. Perhaps, even, for the person at the window, being some place else, then appearing there to peer inside. But, was a hospital in Japan such a disruptive place to be? How does one even know when they need to go to the hospital?

If my pencil were in my ear, I would have used it to write a note on a sheet of Aisopos's paper to place beneath an object heavy enough to both hold the paper in place, and keep the steel door of the building propped open, asking whoever may see it not to close the door while I was out searching for my pencil, which I needed in order to record the relevant dates of Rock Party's potential hospitalization on the calendar. But it wasn't. So I'd have to use a stick to write a note in the snow. I left the apartment and cranked the elevator down to the main floor, where I pushed a cinder block out from beneath a pile of broken fibreboards and over to the door, which I then opened and pushed the cinder block in front of.

Outside, I used my hands to transplant a pile of snow from farther down the wall beside the cinder block and then proceeded to search for a stick. Not finding one, I then tried to find a tree. That's when I realized there were no trees in the immediate vicinity of the former mops, brushes and brooms factory, so I'd have to find a stick-like object instead. Scanning the area, the best thing I could find was one of my own fingers, although I wouldn't be able to write as detailed a snow note with a finger as I would a stick. So, I simply carved out the word *No*, and hoped that would be clear enough.

"Buddy," a guy walking past said. "You okay?"

"Are you going in here?" I asked him.

He looked through the open door.

"Are you okay?" he asked me again. "'Cause you're bleeding."

I looked at the pillowcase wrapped around my arm. It was red.

"Is this not okay?" I asked him.

"I don't know," he said.

"Can I ask you a question?" I said. "Do you think this snow-note makes it clear enough that I don't want this door to close?"

He looked at the snow, then at the door. Then back in the direction he had just come from, as if he had gotten lost.

"You should go to the hospital, man," he said to me.

"If I go to the hospital, do you think people coming and going from this building will know to keep this door propped open?"

He shrugged. "I don't know, probably?"

"Okay." I looked at the pillowcase again. "And you think this is bad?"

"I think. I don't know for certain. That's why I'm saying, man, you should go to the hospital."

I nodded. So that was how you knew when you needed to go to the hospital. A stranger would eventually point it out to you. I looked back down at my snow note. It would have to do.

"Good luck, dude," the guy said as he walked away. "Merry Christmas."

CHAPTER 10

Signs

What was strange about the hospital, at least from where I sat, on a folded-out stretcher in a hallway, pushed up against a wall beside two other folded-out stretchers pushed up against the same wall where other people with open wounds were waiting, was that it was the most quiet place I'd ever been in the entire city. This was where the sirens finally stopped.

A doctor pushed through a door in front of me, then paused, backtracked and closed it again. Through the window, I watched the back of his head nodding as he spoke with the nurse. Then he turned around and looked straight at me. Then opened the door.

"Merry Christmas," he said.

"Why do people keep saying that to me?" I said.

"Are you Jewish?"

"Yes."

He looked at the clipboard in his hand. "Happy Hanukkah, Austin. I'm sorry, I don't know the exact day of it at the moment." He set his clipboard at the foot of the stretcher and took a pair of scissors from the pocket of his white coat. "Which one is it now?"

I didn't answer him, because I didn't know. He opened the scissors at the bottom of the pillowcase and I felt the cold metal press against my arm. Then he cut upward, through the shoelace, until the whole pillowcase opened and began to shed, except for where it was stuck to my arm with blood.

"Is this a pillowcase?" the doctor said.

"Yes."

"That's some real modern war medicine."

"War?"

"Wait here one minute, Austin. You don't have a first aid kit at home?"

He went around a corner and returned afterward with a tray of small medical supplies. Loosening the stuck pillowcase with a soaked cotton ball, he finished removing it from my arm and placed it into a plastic bag, along with his used gloves, and the shoelace that was now technically two, albeit kind of short, but potentially still useful, strings.

"Can I keep those?" I asked him.

"Tell me again what happened here?" he said, as he pulled on a new pair of gloves. "It says glass on your chart. You were playing with glass? What were you doing playing with glass that you would end up this badly cut?"

"I wasn't playing with glass," I said.

"Good to know. Was it glass then, or something else?"

"I don't know where Grear went. She's been closed. Possibly due to Christmas, but possibly worse. My key broke in the lock, so I had to climb through the window above my kitchenette."

"And Grear's what? A friend of yours?"

"I'd say she's a friend to me, but what would you call a person for whom you would knit a sweater?"

"Okay, so you were climbing through a window. Then what happened?"

"The glass had mostly been punched through, except for one small segment that I wasn't aware of."

"Was it you who broke the window?"

"Not originally, but I did break the already broken part some more, yes."

"Where do you live with a window in this condition?"

"888 Dupont."

"Is that a house? Do you live with your parents?"

"An office. My parents are dead."

"I'm sorry. You live in an office?"

"It's not an office anymore. Unless you would consider it to be my office."

"Okay. Well, Austin, look. I'd say we're looking at about eight to ten stitches for this."

The person next to me started gagging. Then screamed. The person next to them screamed in return.

"This is why we recommend that every household have a first aid kit," the doctor continued. "Or in your case, office. So the nurse is going to come and give you some local anesthesia, and I'll be back in about twenty minutes. Do you live alone?"

"Yes."

"After you go home, you'll need to make sure you're monitoring for signs of infection, including fever. The nurse will tell you more. Do you have any next of kin? Maybe someone who could come and pick you up today? It sounds to me like you could use a bit of help."

The nurse came through the same door the doctor had then, followed by another scream from somewhere down that hall, as well as the billowing bottom of a green curtain.

"What's on the other side?" I asked the doctor.

"You're not dying, Austin."

"Of that door."

He looked over his shoulder.

"Patients."

Patients were everywhere, it seemed.

"The only person I know with a car would be Dan, but I don't want Dan to know about this. Perhaps Karly, though. I think she can drive. Can you drive if you're pregnant?"

"Is Karly your next of kin?"

"How do you define 'kin'?"

"A living relative."

"How do you define 'relative'?"

"In this situation, anyone you feel you could call at six a.m. on Christmas morning to pick you up from the hospital after what appears to have been a rough, and kind of weird, night. But if she's Jewish—is she Jewish, too?"

"Yes."

"Even better. Okay, I'll be back in twenty minutes. We'll get you all fixed up."

*

Karly entered through the revolving door like she hated revolving doors. She kicked at it with her big, slipper-like boot, then hit it with her pink puffball keychain. Then, seeing me through the glass, sitting in a chair in the waiting area, looked at me like, *Can you even believe how annoying this door is? Why would they use such a slow-moving piece-of-shit door for the entrance to a hospital? What if I was in labour? And I needed to get inside? Fast? Did they think a pregnant woman with a cervix dilating itself to a million fucking centimetres really needed to be stuck in a revolving door for twenty minutes before checking in to triage? This is definitely the strategic design work of a man. This is the patriarchy—this actual, specific door. And where the hell is Dan to back me up on this? Conveniently absent. As he is in every situation wherein I, his life partner of six years, who is a woman, finds herself being hamster-wheeled by the all-encompassing oppressor that is toxic masculinity. But, whatever. I'm inside now. How are you? Are you okay?*

"Yes," I said.

"Good." She sat down in the chair next to mine. "God, I need to sit down for a minute."

Two paramedics led a stretcher through next, a white sheet covering the entire body. They did not seem to mind waiting for its full revolution.

"Does Dan know?" I asked Karly.

"Yes," she said. "Of course he knows. It's very early in the morning, and I just dropped my bagel and drove off in the car."

"I really didn't want him to know."

"I hear you. You feel uncomfortable with Dan knowing about this situation. Why do you think that is?"

"He's an asshole."

"Is, or can act like one?"

"You're the oldest sibling in your family," I said. "Why didn't you end up with some kind of King Lear complex about it? Or, Queen Lear, I suppose."

"Is that how you feel? Like your brother is King Lear?"

"Yes," I said.

"What happened?"

"I think the tendency to be extra-annoying and controlling originally came from this idea that he had to take care of us all, especially myself, being the youngest. But then it just devolved into this hunger for power."

"To your arm, Austin. How did this happen in the middle of the night?"

"I ended up walking for a really long time after Brad and that other clown left, and then I had that whole conversation with Matilda in the park. Some more time passed, too, while I was trying to sleep under that bit of roof above the entrance to the library, so by the time I climbed up the side of the building and onto the billboard, and then in through the window, it was the middle of the night."

She picked up my hand and held it in hers, her keys pressing into the back of it. To be honest, I could tell she was trying to look me in the eye, but I really didn't want her to know that I knew that. So I kept my own fixed on the sign above the triage desk next to the sign warning us that our abuse would not be tolerated. *Life is full of signs,* it read. *The trick is to know how to read them.*

"You tried to sleep outside the library?" she said.

"Obviously."

"Okay, well, and obviously I don't need to tell you that that's insane. Like, look at yourself. You're in a hospital right now. You don't put your life at risk sleeping in the street, or climbing up a billboard, or whatever. Call."

Then it dawned on me. What if you weren't able to read the sign, because the sign itself was written in Japanese?

"The photos didn't end when they got to the hospital," I said. "They ended when they got to the next life."

Karly sighed.

"No, really. That's it. The ailment or illness wasn't not serious. It was the most serious. It was death-inducing. So the cat was allowed in. Because, why the heck not? What else could have gone wrong at that point? So, for Tacka Attack Love, tomorrow's already happened. Tomorrow was a time in the past. Perhaps, then, *now* is in the future, and thus, the future is *now*. If you can't read the sign, read the images all around you."

Karly let go of my hand and used the puffball to force my face towards her.

"The person in the window was a doctor," I said. "Or a nurse. Or some kind of janitorial, or IT worker. I didn't have my phone."

"This is fucking crazy. You're coming to stay with us for a few days. You can have some breakfast and watch TV. I'll make sure Dan leaves you alone."

At first, I thought maybe Karly was right. Maybe it would be best to spend some time with the people considered to be my next of kin. The idea seemed comforting in that moment, as everything else began to sink in. Dan's bullshit, and then TV, and then a nap. But the very possible fact was that Rock Party was dead. And not only were they a friend of Tacka Attack Love, and some kind of fashionable inspiration to many others, they were also the assumed possessor of the painting of Scoot, and the cat that looked almost exactly like him, and maybe even was him, pre-blinding, paw deformation and fur extraction. So, what happened next? I couldn't figure that out in their newly developed townhouse complex with no wall of clues to interpret.

"I'll take you to your place first, if you need," said Karly. "And make sure you enter the building like a sane person this time."

"I need to go to Walmart."

"I think it's closed. We can take you there on the weekend."

"Someone will be there."

"What do you need?"

"Vindication."

Karly kind of collapsed back in her chair and let her boots pop out from beneath, the toes of which, I realized then, barely grazed the floor. I also realized that, beneath the white feather-stuffed coat that went all the way to her ankles, she was still wearing silk pajamas the exact same shade of purple as the puffball keychain.

"Can I take you to a gas station?" she said.

I shook my head no. "Someone will be there," I said.

*

I ran from the car to the entrance of Walmart. "Yvette," I called through the door, banging on it with the side of my fist. "I know you're in there, Yvette. I know you're in there with that illegal squatter having a very merry Christmas celebration together. Yvette," I continued to yell.

"Stop, Austin," Karly yelled from the car. "Stop it before someone calls the police."

Who was going to call the police? Yvette? No one sleeping in their parked cars in the lot of a closed Walmart on Christmas morning cared about a person shouting and banging on the doors of the store.

"Come down and call the police, Yvette," I, for all intents and purposes, screamed.

"Austin, what the fuck?" Karly yelled. "Who are you screaming at?"

Finally, from the depths of the shopping carts, keys of her red lanyard bouncing off her chest, Yvette emerged, wearing candy cane–striped leggings and a long red T-shirt with a dog on it. The dog was wearing antlers. Yvette was also wearing antlers. She yelled through the door that the store was closed.

"Why are you dressed like that at the place where you work?" I yelled back. "Are those pajamas?"

"I said, we're closed," she yelled again.

"I know what you're doing in there," I yelled. "I know about the Cheetos and the stains. I know about the criminal you're harbouring."

She gave me the stink eye. "You need to leave. Now."

"Or what?" I yelled.

"Or I'm calling the cops," she yelled back.

I banged on the door with both fists.

"You aren't even supposed to be here. You're in there playing house in the pet department with that freaky man-thing while Rock Party is dead, and so is Fasóli, and Sarah's at Aisopos's home right now caring for her orchid. Sarah. Who you fired. Whose fish is also dead. And one day, Yvette, you'll be dead too. Is this how you want to be remembered? As some orange fingerprint stain on an otherwise basic tacky pajama shirt?"

At that point, I opened my eyes, which I hadn't realized I'd closed. Yvette had taken a few steps backward from the door and was holding her phone up by her shoulder, like a threat. But she didn't look threatened in the face. Just stinky-eyed still. I felt a hand on my back.

"Get in the car," Karly said.

I turned around and walked away with her.

"Don't tell Dan about this," I said. "Don't tell Dan I stressed the baby."

"My baby's fine, Austin," she said. "I'm fine, too. And so are you. You are an inherently fine person, and this is all going to end soon."

*

I didn't know what Karly meant by that. That this was all going to end. Yvette's employment? I seriously doubted Yvette would ever give up that red lanyard. And the kaftan man was going nowhere until, at the very earliest, spring. Would Aisopos stop receiving packages from Greece? Would Hadir leave his basement? Or perhaps Tacka Attack Love would finally find the words to explain the origin of BadDog's painting and therefore its subject, Scoot? Regardless, there, in the passenger seat of her and Dan's idling car, in the laneway behind the building where I lived, the door of which was still propped open with a cinder block, Karly did not elaborate. She only asked me who that woman was in the store, how I knew she was there and why I was yelling the things I was yelling about death.

That was the woman who fired Sarah—a middleman of sorts between the distributor of Neofinetia orchids and cat treats from Missouri. She instructs people to stock these products upon shelves. Tacka Attack's orchid is in memory of her friend, Rock Party, and Aisopos's is for his *glykó fasóli*, who was also from Japan, where Tacka Attack is now, and where the memory of Rock Party thus remains alive. So, what is Yvette's motive in harbouring a potential animalist criminal seeking to threaten the well-being of a person as kind, attentive and beautiful as Sarah? Who only wants to earn a living so she can pay the rent to maintain the foundation upon which she can grow and enjoy her other various talents, such as band-forming and leading? A cut of reward? And did she leave her greasy fingerprints on the package of treats I'd bought for Scoot on purpose? To send me a message? That, for some reason, I was next? Next for what? And why me, anyway? The only thing connecting myself, Austin, to Tacka, Rock Party, Aisopos and Sarah was my broken heart.

"I've pieced a lot of things together," I told Karly. "But there are still some things that are going to drive me crazy. And also, right now, I feel very sad for Tacka Attack Love."

"What's Tacka Attack Love?" she said.

"An ASMR specialist from Japan, whom I met through Hadir, whom he met through his dumb game that he plays online all day and all night long."

"What happened to her that's made you so sad?"

"Her friend died. I think she cared for them. Literally. I think she would go to them in the hospital and bring their pet cat to them, and do ASMR to soothe their body and mind. I think she took them for walks in the garden and treated them to tapioca juice. And before they went to the hospital, I think they would walk on the beach in Fukuoka together, and as someone who knows what it's like to have a friend who walks with you, even on very snowy days, even when the path has been completely buried in gross trash, it makes me feel very sad."

I didn't mean to make Karly cry.

"Please don't tell Dan I made you cry," I said.

She laughed through her tears. "Are you coming for breakfast?"

"No," I said.

"Wait—where's your car?"

I didn't answer. She nodded and looked away from me, out the window beside her, and wiped her teary eyes. But then she whipped back around and kind of hit me upside the back of the head in a manner very similar to Hadir's.

"You need to be more careful," she yelled. "I never want to go back to that place. Ever. I hate it there."

"You have to have your baby, though," I said.

"Well, I wish I was having a water birth."

"So have one."

"No. I can't. We're not talking about me. You don't need to be some kind of hero, or whatever it is you're trying to be. This is what happens."

*

I left Karly that morning wondering, for the second time, what she had meant by the word "this," until I'd cranked myself up to my apartment and found the notice of eviction on the floor in front of it. My tenancy? Was that the ending she was referring to? Then, what is that which "happens"?

And who would evict someone during Hanukkah?

Inside, I tacked the notice to the absolute right of everything else; the calendar, the pencilled calendar, the original article on BadDog's mural from *Japan Views Lifestyle News in English*, the contest information and ten biographies of the ten different Japanese contestants of it, BadDog's included, directions from Fukuoka to Tokyo, Toronto to Tokyo, Toronto to Fukuoka via Tokyo, and Fukuoka to Taitō Ward, the map of clues shaped like Japan, information about the Missouri Botanical Gardens, the Wikipedia entry on ASMR, the original note written by Rock Party beneath their photo and copied by myself, Grear's translation of the note, the origami cat containing Matilda's phone number, the names *Bubbleheaven2*, *Aisopos* and *Her*, Scoot's package of cheese-stained cat treats, Karly's flipped business card and the rectangle encompassing the question *Who?*, then removed the shoelace from my second shoe and looped it from the eviction notice to the drawing of that window. Had I found my pencil instead of going to the hospital,

I would have crossed out that question and written a new word—*Doctor*—with an asterisk, of course, while keeping the question mark as it was. What "happens" was still a question mark.

But I hadn't found my pencil. Instead, I'd found myself in the same place as Rock Party (whose real name was Tenchi) as well as their cat, and Tacka Attack Love (the patter of that cat). Had I not, I wouldn't have discovered this very significant change of word, or this preservation of the unknown. This picture of Rock Party in the garden, un-costumed, wielding no fancy stick, was them as they truly were—as well as all the people who'd ever admired that picture were—succumbing.

I'm sorry, I messaged Tacka Attack Love.

Then the message disappeared and the screen turned black. Dan was calling. I waited until he stopped. A moment later, he called again. Then, sent a message:

Why aren't you answering?

Again, I waited until the message disappeared, then went back to my own message for Tacka.

Tomorrow is in the future, I told her.

Dan: *What the hell happened?*

Me: *It doesn't matter.*

Dan: *Yes it does.*

Me: *It really doesn't though.*

Dan: *What happened this morning? Why did Karly have to come get you from the hospital?*

He tried calling again. Still, I didn't answer.

Why did Tenchi dress up in those outfits and pose for photos so often? I asked Tacka.

Tenchi Sword Play.

Dan: *If you don't answer me I'm calling the cops.*

Me: *I'm not sure if you understand what cops are for.*
Did a lot of people love Tenchi's costumes?
Dan: *Cops are for people like you*
Yes, she said.
Dan: *people who lie and hide stuff*
Dan: *from their families and who pose potential threats to the safety of others*
Dan: *and to themselves*
Dan: *and are probably even doing something illegal without realizing it*
Dan: *because they are too retarded to know any better.*
I waited.
Who takes care of Tenchi's cat now?
Dan: *Answer me. Did you try to kill yourself?*

Why was Dan always assuming the worst of me? Why was he so concerned about my presence around Karly, and why was he always, almost every single day, messaging me? Dan, you stupid jerk-off, I did not try to kill myself. I simply climbed into my apartment through the window, which resulted in a basic yet deep enough gash on my right arm that it plainly necessitated eight to ten straightforward stitches, the procedure of which to acquire them being super elementary. I would never put the eight, possibly nine, or even ten people that would notice I was gone through that which the hundreds, possibly tens of hundreds of fans of Rock Party's photos have had to go through since their very unfortunate and very sad departure from Instagram.

Cat have.
Have equalled go.
Me: *I'm alive today. Is that good enough for you?*

CHAPTER 11

When All That Remains Is Dust and Dust Will Never Truly Leave Anyway

Cat have where?

Yes, replied Tacka, as though she did not know the meaning of the word "where."

Cat have there?

Cat have here?

Cat have near?

Beach Fukuoka. Woods, she said.

Which was it? Beach, or woods? And also, *where* wasn't even an auxiliary verb. It was an adverb. Every time I thought I'd deduced the course of her logic, wouldn't Tacka Attack Love go and tack on a new contradiction? How could BadDog have found this cat, then, if he was in Taitō Ward, Tokyo, and it was some place in Fukuoka, which was 197 hours away by foot? Was that not a lot of hours? It seemed like it. But perhaps it wasn't. Perhaps time and distance are different to a person who has consciously unconfined themselves from the rationale of their own humanity, including comprehension of our standard modes of measurement. Still, though, did that mean he was capable of not only seeing, but potentially dismembering and then creating a painting of an animal on the other end of the country? Could BadDog transcend space? Could Scoot?

No. That could not be possible. There had to be an empirical explanation. For example, the cat belonging to Tenchi, otherwise known as Rock Party, may not, in fact, have been Scoot, but a look-a-like of him, apart from its intact eyes, limbs and fur. The look-a-like may also have enjoyed perching in the exact way Scoot probably would have perched in this moment that just happened to resemble the moment that was captured in BadDog's painting. Or, of course, BadDog may have transported himself from Tokyo to Fukuoka—via bus, plane, train, ferry or feet, where he came into contact with the pet of a dead Instagram star, a pet that would go on to become the dead pet of a new Instagram user: me. Whether on the beach, or in the woods, or elsewhere, these assumed whereabouts of the cat at this present moment were just that—assumptions—presumed by Tacka Attack Love. But why, then, would he leave the place where his art, and therefore his inferred livelihood, was located, just to travel to a place to find himself an animal, the likes of which there would almost certainly be plenty within his immediate vicinity?

The other possibility was, of course, that the cat would have found its own way from Fukuoka to Taitō Ward, Tokyo, either by walking, or scooting between the open doors of a bus and several trains, a plane and many several subway cars, or a ferry, which would have also, in all probability, included the crossing of a ramp. In my experience with Scoot, it had appeared that he was, in all likelihood, in search of a place to rest—a place with consistent access to a comfortable bed corner, a heap of warm clothing and treats manufactured in, and shipped from, Missouri. In other words, a home. So why would he leave the one he already had?

I was barely wading in the water at that point. Most of my body was numb, anyway. I thought of what my face might look like, tilted back as far as I could tilt it in order to keep my chin above the surface. Blue and very white, like that of a white napkin that had gotten a little wet. When I looked to the beach, it was still empty. But when I closed my eyes and dreamed of the beach, there was Tacka, faceless, sitting on the wet sand. As if it had been following her, Tenchi's cat appeared and hopped onto her lap. Snow was falling and forming little cone-like piles on both of their heads. I could feel it on my face, too, which had probably, by then, turned translucent because of it. I supposed it would have been possible for Scoot to want to leave for the sake of leaving. And after having been gone for some time, he might have then wanted to return. Perhaps, for an animal, there is no here or there, only, simply, varying degrees of comfort.

*

When I woke up, it was quiet. The streets outside were quiet. As were the pipes inside. Was it the effect of Christmas? I wasn't sure, but people still needed urgent care during holidays. People still needed to run water and heat the rooms they were in.

This was the effect of being alone. And also, perhaps, of being Jewish. But mostly, of being alone. Potentially, even, the only person inside the entire site of the soon-to-be-luxury condominiums, and former mops, brushes and brooms factory. Did I want to message Tacka Attack Love then? Kind of. She was the only person who came to mind when I thought about who there was out there that was left to talk to. But even Ronda had disappeared. I waved my phone above my face. I got out of the bed and waved it near the wall behind the nightstand. Then the wall beside that wall. Was it possible her signal was unable to pass through all the tacked-up papers? I moved closer to the kitchenette. I even tried the washroom.

Finally, I opened the door and took a step into the hallway. I held out the phone in both directions. Then I crouched down and held it near the floor. Finally she reappeared, an *i* enclosed within a circle where her fan of bars would normally be. What did this mean? Did she have information to share with me? I stood back up, facing the elevator door. I'd never travelled to any floor other than the one leading outside and the one I lived on. Those were the points where the crank stopped turning. Did this elevator even go anywhere else? How would one know when to stop turning and step off? It was dark in there. How big might the gaps between the elevator platform and the other floors be? This one was about half a foot. You needed to be prepared.

There had to be stairs somewhere. There were other doors. Certainly, at least one of them led to a different floor. Those who conducted their work within the offices must have, at some point, necessitated witness to the goings-on within other sectors of production. They may have been the ones calling the shots financially, but surely, it was the assemblers and fabricators of the mops, brushes and brooms who were truly running the show. What if they'd decided they were angry, hungry, gave in one day and gnawed the wooden handles into spearheads with which to forcefully take over the entire operation from those sipping tap water from mugs on the floor above? What if they were to become ravenous? Or, simply, just stopped working?

Behind the first door I had cupped my ear against was an apparent silence, a dusty one, like it had been there for a long, long time. Around the corner, the next door also sounded like it blocked nothing. I tried the knob. It was unlocked. So I opened the door and, with the exception of an art easel propped dead centre in the room, I was right. No sink or refrigerator. Not even a barber stool. I switched the light on beside the door and found red footprints and globs of dried paint splattered across the floor. Squatting to get a closer look, I could see it was all coated in a layer of dust. The only disruption to the scene were my own fingerprints, and, after backing out of the doorframe, the prints of my shoes.

I continued down the hall until it turned again, and I found myself facing a third door, this one leading into the centre of the building. Again, I cupped my ear and listened. It sounded hollow. A slight knocking. Like the whole space was just one giant pipe. Was that possible? I lifted the metal bar that crossed the door horizontally from its catch, and leaned it against the wall. It felt as though it hadn't been opened since the mid-century and had, over time, melded itself to its frame. The strength of my arms alone could not open it. Neither that of my shoulders and torso. So I picked up the metal bar and used its strength. The door dislodged with the first knock, and that was how I found myself at the top of a winding metal staircase, gazing downward into what must have been the belly of the former mops, brushes and brooms factory.

The floor was just as dust-covered as the artist's studio had been. The walls looked like they were shedding. Stacked in a heap against one wall were wooden poles, along with some other wooden boards that looked like they'd been burned in the blackened spot on the floor that looked like it had been set on fire, and garbage bags with what appeared to be soiled clothing, as well as actual garbage, spilling out. Near that heap, a black steel machine that looked like its job was, at one point, to shred things into little bits, then spit those bits back out, was bolted to the floor. There were fingerprints on the handle of its arm.

I looked up. Other than mine, there were no other footprints. No other breathing sounds, either, as far as I could hear. I looked at my hand. Had I been the one to turn this handle? Or set, then subsequently put out, that fire? Was I the criminal who spray-painted that seemingly indiscernible lime-green message on the wall beside that door over there? *Dig gugorcug. Die euenorue.* Whatever it was I was possibly trying to tell myself, I hoped it had nothing to do with what was on the other side. I went over to it.

Upon opening the door, I found myself in another hall, standing directly across from what appeared to be a public washroom. I crossed the hall into the washroom, and tried the flusher on a urinal. Nothing happened. Why would the water run in my office, but not here in the workers' washroom? Was there a clog? I tried the foot pump below the communal sink. Again, no water, but a bubbling, followed by a burp from the large drain in the centre of the floor. Then, what sounded like a giggle. Was something down there, living in the pipes below these cracked and broken tiled floors? Was there something alive, or not alive, inside of that one locked stall?

I sprinted from the washroom and rounded the corner to the adjoining hall, where two single doors were located at either end. From the furthest, light peeked out below the bottom. Some noise, as well, like talking, shouting, even, rose and fell. As I got closer, it became clear that these were the sounds of a television. I cupped my ear to the door. It sounded like *Judge Judy*. Was it? It was. Had I seen this episode? The sound switched abruptly to the laughter of a studio audience, and then to what sounded like the growling of a wrestling match. I checked my phone for a Wi-Fi signal. For the first time, Ronda had three bold bars. This was her home. This was where she lived. And she was into wrestling. I tapped to connect.

You were a liar and untrusting?

Lied? Lied about what? I'd never lied to Tacka Attack Love. I'd been honest from the very beginning, from the inauguration of my Instagram account, just as Sarah had advised for me to be. Was it something on the wall? Everything tacked there was factual information. I was simply collecting and attempting to organize it into a cohesive narrative. And untrusting? I trusted Tacka, even though practically nothing she said made any sense in English. I found the sense. Why did she feel this way? Had I lost her now, too? Cutlery clinked against a plate, and there was a shuffling along the floor.

I crouched down to my hands and knees, then all the way onto my stomach, so as to peer beneath the door. Ronda had large feet and wore flip-flops. Her toenails looked like jagged grey bones, and her heels were the colour of corn-coloured wool. Her ankles were bare, but became very hairy, curly and black, an inch or so up the calf. I could hear the sound of water trickling. It seemed that she was washing her dishes. I sniffed the air between us. It smelled like hot dogs. To be honest, in that moment, my tongue tasted like I was tasting her foot, and her foot tasted like a hot dog.

The phone dinged in my hand. Ronda's feet went still. The water stopped, and she turned in my direction. Who would even be sending me a text message right now, on Christmas Day night, when any living person with knowledge of my phone number was either feeling hurt by me, distrustful of me, was distrustful themselves, in my opinion, mysteriously disappeared, or somewhat Christian?

Hey why u call the other day? Butt dial?

Gunner. Ronda took a few steps forward. The wrestling stopped, too. I held my breath.

Hows it going long time no talk?

I pushed up from the floor and began speed-walking, then sprinting, again, back in the direction I'd come. As I rounded the corner toward the washroom, though, I couldn't help but glance back at her apartment. That was how I finally met the real Ronda. Naked from the waist down, penis dangling between her hairy legs, red windbreaker zipped up to her chin.

*

I cannot confirm whether or not the stairwell leading to the former-manufacturing-centre-turned-bonfire-pit, which in turn led to the floor of the building from where a partial nudist disguised as a Wi-Fi signal named Ronda had been emanating for many years now, ended one or two storeys below the floor upon which I lived. I cannot confirm whether or not there was another flight of stairs leading from Ronda's floor to any other floor, above or below an exit, or an entrance. I didn't know what was behind the first door neighbouring mine, who it was that once lived in the artist's studio, or what it was they potentially created in there. I didn't know if there were any ghouls inhabiting the washroom or clogging the pipes below it. If ghouls travelled through hidden stairwells or elevator shafts, I also wouldn't know if one had entered my apartment, because as far as I understood, they turned the air cold with their presence, and by now the cold air coming through the window I'd broken had reached every corner of my apartment, another quandary for which I did not have the scientific knowledge to solve, other than to continue to wear my coat and huddle against the radiator. These were not the mysteries that made me feel like I was in a strange new old place, however. These were not the reasons why, on a holiday I didn't celebrate, I was both sad and very frightened.

It was the wall. This wall which, covered from right to left, was not a series of miscellaneous yet interconnected clues. It did not explain why, and how, an anomalous cat, worth much reward, had shown up at my door, when I could barely get in and out of the building myself. It did not tell me where he came from, and it did not tell me where Hadir, Sarah, Grear, Dan, Karly, Brad or Kirk had all gone. Who were Tacka Attack Love and Matilda before Scoot's death? Who were Glykó Fasóli and Rock Party, before each becoming memorialized as a Neofinetia orchid?

I stepped away from the radiator and picked up the hockey stick. This was a mural. And it needed to be destroyed.

What I can confirm is this: Although there do been times in my life when I lied, to you, I never did (Will? May?). I can do regrets, who could not? The painting, the contest, the orchids, the tapioca juice, it was all real. Is real. Only the cat is not. He is dust now. But, to far to I am aware, dust lasts a long time. It might last forever. I cannot know if it is water soluble, but I will search for the answer to that after.

U know what I was thinking about? Like two days ago. Like yesterday. Remember u me hadir we drove out to that place near the airport & went go karting. Man that was good times. Haha hadir was like a mental. Haha we should do that again. I'm free like every weekend basically except this weekend and next. Want to?

R.I.P. SCOOT

Austin—I'm sorry I have yet to respond to your last message. I've been working double shifts at Nordstrom, where I took a last-minute job wrapping gifts. The person I replaced stole a watch mere minutes before I'd shown up with a resume in hand. I guess you could say I had found myself in the right place at the right time? Would you say that? Without any intended pun? Anyway, it's over now, the job, despite my suggestion to management that they continue the service year-round.

I miss u guys i love u guys.

People really light up from the inside out when handed a well-wrapped box.

I picked a dead louse from the washroom floor and placed it on my phone screen. Then blew it away. Is dust water soluble? I searched. No. In fact, sometimes, it becomes clouds. Other times, it doesn't.

Dust is not water soluble, I let Tacka know.

Hi Austin, how are you feeling? How is your arm?

Would you still like to borrow my computer?

If you're going to choose to be unmannerly and really weird, then I'm going to stop reaching out to you, bud.

Cat is a her.

You can be a loner forever, no nieces or nephews, who cares.

WHEN ALL THAT REMAINS IS DUST AND DUST WILL NEVER TRULY LEAVE ANYWAY

Cat is a her?

He was a he.

He is a her. Cat is a her. ASMR? Some later?

He was a he.

No. That is all. Thank you, Tacka Attack Love.

CHAPTER 12

The Winner

In the morning, there was a knock at the door. I crawled out from the washroom. Through the space that was once a window with a hole in it, I saw blue sky. As well, some actual sunlight. Because of it, the glass granules across the kitchenette floor sparkled. The papers scattered over the floor were all aflush. Even the package of cat treats amongst the pile seemed to wink up at me, if I tilted my head to my shoulder. Why would it be winking? What was this yellow envelope half-stuffed beneath the door?

I crawled over to the door and opened it. There was no one in the hall. No sound of a cable moving through pulleys from the elevator shaft. I touched the envelope. It was bubbled. Cosmo Music—The Musical Instrument Superstore! I sat back on my heels and tore the envelope open with my teeth. Then I tipped it, and out fell another envelope, smaller, and square. *Cosmo Strings!* it read across the front. Beneath many papers, the guitar was face down on the floor. Like I'd just left it there. Like I didn't know how to treat it. Or paper. *That's not how I feel about you,* I thought about the guitar. But do thoughts even matter when directed toward guitars? *I also don't hold any resentment toward any of you,* I thought about the papers. *I just don't need you, after all.* I looked at Aisopos's box, sitting there, waiting to be useful. *When I return you today, please know it isn't personal. Perhaps, even, you'll be happy to go home?*

*

The steel door to the former factory was as I'd left it—propped open. The snow note, however, had mostly melted. Box in a one-armed tow, I went to Grear's. The open sign was hung on the door. Once she saw me standing in front of it, she came out from behind the counter to let me in.

"You need more help with your mystery?" she said.

I sort of dropped the box at my feet, then kicked it forward.

"No, in fact, I need to transport this all the way back to Aisopos's house, the house in which Sarah resides. Somehow."

"Okay." She pulled the box farther in.

"I thought you went some place similar to Bali?" I said.

"Bali?" She stuck out her tongue. "Yuck. You, come sit."

I followed her over to the counter, where I finally took her up on the van seat behind it. On the television, Billy was hanging off the side of a cliff.

"What happened?" I said.

He fell.

"Grear?" I said. "Did Billy just die?"

The electric kettle clicked. She poured boiled water over a bowl of ramen while looking above her glasses to the screen. "They never really die," she said, handing me the bowl, then held up her hand to block a light beam reflecting off the seat buckle beside me. "Ack," she said. "Too sunny today."

"Yes," I said.

"Sky's almost blue, for Chrissake."

I wound the fork in the noodles. "I can pay my tab today, Grear. If you happen to accept phone credit cards."

"I don't," she said.

"Well, the guitar strings arrived today. Once I've finished returning this box of paper, I'll be able to restring the guitar, and take it to the pawnshop. By the way, did someone stop in to purchase a sink trap?"

"Yep."

Terrifying.

"You go out with your girlfriend today?" she asked.

"Mm." I couldn't lie. I knew that, in returning the box to Aisopos's house, there was also a chance that I would potentially have an encounter with Sarah. In fact, she was likely the person who would help him open the door. And while she was so kind as to offer her computer, she may still have felt that, given the circumstances, the most appropriate thing to do would have been to drop it off, then leave to run an errand, or go to an interview, returning only to pick it up afterward, or stay, but just for the duration of its use, which would only have been for a maximum of fifteen minutes, and not nearly enough time to reduce the tension between us to a comfortable amount.

In other words, the days of our going out may have ended the day I left her in tears, which had somewhat erased the delicate curve at the end of the simple yet alluring line of black eyeliner she had applied to her eyelids that morning. And while clearly she was still very capable of securing employment with or without it, she had chosen her outfit, and its corresponding makeup, for a reason. It made her feel a certain way. And I, a person whom up to that point she had believed she could trust not to spoil such feelings, had gone and done just that.

"You can eat?" asked Grear.

I lifted the knot of noodles to my mouth.

"But no girlfriend?" she said.

"There are some things I don't know right now, Grear," I said. "For instance, how a man could survive a fall from a very high cliff, or why it's the women who end up on the lam, and not the sociopaths who drive them out. I don't know what, if any, type of role I've played in the artistic war against animal, or human, cruelty. I may have been cruel. I hope I haven't. But my house is cold, and possibly toxic. I had no plan for when the first bag of food ran out. And at the end of the day, it was my decision to allow the vet to take the life of Scoot. So I don't think I deserve the sum he was worth."

Grear tossed me a new key.

"I'm going to have to move soon," I told her.

"Yep. We all of us do here in the plaza."

"I'm going to become a condo."

She fanned her hands in front of us as if to say, *Picture this*.

"Car park," she said.

*

Aisopos was on his couch watching television. I dropped the box in front of the door, then went around to knock on the window.

"Hey," I yelled. He looked over at me. "Can I come in?"

He shrugged. I pointed to the didgeridoo leaned beside him.

"Get Sarah."

He shook his head no. So I went back around to the steps and tried the door myself. It was unlocked.

"The door's open," I called inside. "Is it okay if I come in?"

No answer.

"Okay, here I come," I said, kicking the box into the neat lineup of Sarah's various footwear, plus one bright white and seemingly hardly worn pair of men's sneakers.

"Aisopos," I said, from the bottom step leading up into the living room. "I'm becoming concerned that the stitches holding my skin together might be coming loose from carrying this box which I'd like to return to you today, as well as give thanks to you for loaning me in the first place. So I'm going to leave it here, below this step, and when my arm has healed, I will come back and move it into its original place within the cold room."

While Aisopos just stared at me, I listened for any sound of Sarah within the house that would indicate she'd overheard. Unless she was also listening? Aisopos shook his head no.

"She's not?"

No.

"Is she even here?"

"Nope."

"You can talk, then?"

He shrugged.

"I figured it out. Rock Party is with Fasóli. And Scoot. And Sarah's dead fish, and boyfriend. And my parents."

He nodded yes, as if he already knew.

"Did you already know that?"

He looked over to the cabinet. Was the story of the future contained there, as well?

"Would you mind if I see the bowl again?" I asked.

"Go," he waved.

I went over and picked it up from the bottom shelf. "It's a pretty thing," I said.

"Take it."

"I have a mug at my apartment I can use. And three skillets."

"It's for the cat."

"My cat is dead. Remember?"

He waved again.

"Nah," he said. "The next one. It's coming."

It's coming?

"Aisopos, what are in these parcels beside the bowls?"

He shrugged.

"You don't know what it is you keep receiving every three weeks by ship from Greece?"

He circled his hands, like maybe he did, or maybe he didn't know.

"Can I open one?"

"Bah," he said, as in, I assumed, go for it. So I set down the bowl on the coffee table and picked up the topmost parcel from the shelf, breaking open the cardboard seal. Inside was a stack of paper, the initials *A.G.* imprinted in bold capital lettering at the top of each sheet.

"Paper?"

Aisopos gestured for me to bring it to him. I handed him a sheet and he examined it top to bottom, turning it over it in his large, dry hands.

"Hah!" he said, surprised.

"You're surprised by this?" I asked him.

"Yep," he said.

I looked back at the stack of parcels, counting, then not bothering to count anymore.

"There are so many of these parcels," I said. "For how long have they been coming?"

He circled a hand again, but this time, like he was drawing an infinity sign.

"You know you could just get paper from Walmart, right?"

He waved a finger at me.

"Nah," he said. Then rubbed the *A.G.* "See?"

I turned back to the shelves of Aisopos's life story. He must have been promoted at some point and worked in the office of the factory. He must have used a fax machine and wrote letters with the pen positioned next to the piece of black steel.

"Maybe you could ask Sarah to use her computer to help you end your subscription to this stationery service?" I said. "I'm sure she wouldn't mind."

"Eh." He shrugged.

Maybe he would, maybe he wouldn't.

*

I did take the bowl. Because, why not? You never know what a person may or may not be able to foretell. And I supposed I'd have to leave the mug where I'd found it when I moved. It wouldn't hurt to have another dish. Though it did feel quite cold in my hands. Whether or not this was due to the exposure of its ceramic material to the chilled air of the day after Christmas Day, or because the bowl harboured the ghoul of Glykó Fasóli, I didn't know, but I liked to think that, in either case, what the bowl represented was goodness; I felt stronger holding the bowl, protected somehow. Yo-yos could technically crack it, yes. As could a beak. The butt of an unyieldingly pointed toe. But, as far as I was aware, ceramic didn't shatter the way glass did, for instance. So in those situations, I would maintain the broken pieces. And even those broken pieces of my personal tapioca bowl would be pieces of a personal tapioca bowl. Pieces of goodness. Sizeable, and sharp.

As I pushed the cinder block back inside, the sunlight lighting the floor and walls of the former mops, brushes and brooms factory shrunk fast until disappearing completely behind the closing steel door. After a moment, my eyes adjusted to their normally dark space, and I was able to see the elevator again, with which to crank myself up.

The door to my apartment was pulled over but not completely shut. Had I left it that way? I nudged it forward with my bowl, and peered inside. As far as I could see, which was past the section of the paper-covered floor where Scoot had initially curled himself upon my sweater, the foot portion of the bed, the washroom door and through to the kitchenette, there was no one else inside. With another nudge, I was able to fit my head all the way through the gap in order to see around the door, which encompassed the remainder of the paper-covered floor, and the head portion of the bed. There was no one there, either. Someone may have been on the other side of the door itself, but when I kicked it the rest of the way open, it simply swung until it hit the wall. I opened the washroom door in the same way, with a kick, and it also hit the wall. When I kicked the shower curtain, my foot did.

But someone had been inside of my apartment that day. Someone had entered through the open steel door, taken the elevator on their own to the third floor, and let themselves in, after potentially receiving no answer from their gentle, heartbeat-like knock. Because there, on the formerly empty spot on the nightstand, erstwhile sitting spot of treat-hunting Scoot and original setting of light-producing lamp, was a container of probably okay bean-like cookies. I opened the lid. They appeared to have been cut in the shape of bells. I took a bite of one, holding the bowl against my chest to catch the crumbs. It did taste like a bean. But it was okay.

What I noticed next, though, was that beneath the container, in a way that seemed as though it were being pinned down by it in order to prevent it from being carried away and lost amongst the mess upon the floor should a breeze travel through the open space above the kitchenette sink, was a single sheet of paper. I pulled it out. The biography of one entrant to the art contest—Makiko Ide, twenty-three, student at Musashino Art University.

I turned to face the wall. The only thing left upon it was the calendar, drawn in pencil, which could not be erased by the blade of a hockey stick. Did I even want to know if, in fact, today was the day designated by the judges of the contest as later? After everything I had heretofore been through in the name of art and money? I laid the paper on the bed. Next to it, I set the tapioca bowl, and next to that, the container of cookies. I trusted Sarah. If she had gone so far as to enter my apartment in a technically illegal manner, sift through the demolished mural upon the floor to find the biography of Makiko Ide, and intentionally arrange it, along with her cookies, for me to discover, there must have been a reason. Sarah would not just do things without first reasoning. So, I removed my phone from my jacket pocket, connected to that fraud Ronda, searched the article on BadDog from *Japan Views Lifestyle News in English*, scrolled to the bottom of it, and tapped the link to the contest. An announcement had been posted regarding the contest winner, and the runners-up.

Makiko Ide, a twenty-three-year-old student at Musashino Art University, had earned the grand prize of twenty-five thousand yen, as well as the opportunity to take part in a group exhibition at Hōnto No Kimochi Gallery and Café in Setagaya City, Tokyo, Japan, with her submission, "Painting of a Photo of a Beach." Below a photograph of Makiko was a small image of the painting itself. A simple beach, portrayed from the perspective of a person standing just off the shore of it, looking down at their feet in the water.

I closed the announcement and opened the Instagram profile of Tacka Attack Love. I tapped the most recent photo she'd shared of her own feet in the water at the beach in Fukuoka, then tapped the name of the second person who had liked it—@maki18892. But nothing happened. Maki18892 had a private account. The only way for me to learn anymore about them, it seemed, was to tap a request button, which I immediately did. Moments later, she appeared. Maki18892 lived in Tokyo, Japan. She liked arcade games, having very tiny people painted onto her nails, and sitting on a wall at the bottom of the steps of the MAU library, from where she could peacefully sip through the straw of a metallic gold cup, personalized by the charm of a single bronze coin.

Her same 23.

Her Tokyo.

MAU.

Her had won the contest.

But, now what?

*

Without snow, my search for Sarah's footprints was turning up nothing but cigarette butts, dog pee, dog poo and several torn-open packages of Ho Hos smushed into the ground, resembling dog poo. So the only path of hers I could reason would be next to, and around, all of that stuff, and hopefully travelling in the direction of her rented room at Aisopos's house via laneway to the main road, north on the sixth street west, and through the backyard.

I was right. And luckily, on the sixth street, Sarah had paused about halfway up, it appeared, to admire a bush. I paused to admire her, still far enough away that she had yet to notice me. She picked something off the bush. Then admired that thing, now in her palm. I couldn't take it anymore. I started to sprint toward her. But what was I going to say? I hadn't thought of anything before starting to run.

"What did you find?" I called out.

She looked up, then waited for me to catch up to her before responding. I caught up. She displayed her palm.

"Mulberries. I can't believe they're still here," she said.

To be honest, it looked like it had barely ripened in the first place.

"Unbelievable," I said.

"It's inconceivable. I could make jam with them."

After noting this, however, she tossed the berry to a patch of broken pavement. What was I going to say next?

"You came back."

"I could never leave this place," she said. "Tell me everything."

Everything? My last key broke, and I tried to sleep outside the library. I received stitches in my arm after breaking back into my apartment, in the process of which I discovered that the *cat asmr good japan* video was filmed in the Fukuoka hospital, where Rock Party was, until they died. I discovered what ASMR actually was. I discovered I was being evicted. I tried to avenge your unjust firing from Walmart, and I tried to intentionally yet inadvertently see you today at Aisopos's house upon returning his box of fax paper. In the end, Makiko Ide did win the art contest, as you so rightly pointed out, even amongst the disaster I'd created, and did so with nothing but a simple, even, I'll just say it, boring beach.

"What do you do when the thing that you've put everything into takes you nowhere in the end?" I asked her.

She pursed her entire face into a thought for me. It was so pursed, it was an arrow. Then she took my hand in hers, and together, we started walking. The sky wasn't blue anymore, it was grey again, and already seemed to be turning dark. I wasn't sure if we were going to go to Aisopos's house, or the former mops, brushes and brooms factory, or neither, and just out. Regardless, she kept a slow, unwavering pace, unconcerned entirely with the clip-clop of stilts approaching from behind.

"Change things," she finally said. "Then do your best all over again."

I sensed the stirring of wings opening behind our shoulders, and smelled the scent of sour fruit as he opened his mouth to caw. It was no coincidence that, through the simple act of guiding me forward, Sarah could course through my hand, arm, across my chest, up my neck, and all around my head and face. She was right—she could never leave this place; she was a part of it. Wherever she was, that space was hers. The Birdman stomped.

"Where will I live?" I asked her.

As I let her, she let me in.

EPILOGUE

Aisopos Tells Us Everything

Ken, father of Tenchi, is one day trying to sweep. But, the cat is very annoying. It will not move from beneath the zataku. It hisses to Ken. It's yowling. *Dumb cat*, thinks Ken. *It's Tenchi cat. Should be the problem of Tenchi*. But, Tenchi lives in the hospital now. So Ken's got no choice. He tips the zataku. Opens the door. Sweeps the cat out. *I don't know; cat has a cat issue, needs to do its cat thing. Go be natural, cat.* Ken did not notice its bloated stomach, or swollen nipples. Ken did not notice such extra licking of its anus and vulva.

Close by to Ken and Tenchi's home is a beach. There, near wood of pines, cat makes a cozy nest in silver grass and driftwood. Surprise, it gives birth to five kittens. Four kittens do the normal kitten thing. Open up their eyes, blue. Get coordinated. Mew. Fifth kitten, though. Nope. Fifth is born deformed, blind. Runt. Cat gives it extra licking, extra milk. But, cat has to take care of the healthy ones first. So, soon drags runt into the sand. Then carries the four good kittens back to Ken and Tenchi's home. Who cares. It will feed an eagle or boar or something. Natural.

R.I.P. SCOOT

*

Twelve weeks later, Ken sells one kitten to a family. Two get out, join a cat gang. The last one Ken gives up to the old gardener neighbour, Yasushi. In exchange, Yasushi gives Ken a beautiful orchid. Ken and cat think, *That's that then.* Cat thinks, *Runt's long time dead by now.* But, runt is not. Runt was not found by an eagle or boar. Instead, by a girl, Makiko, friend of Tenchi, during one day as she goes walking along the beach.

Makiko soon moves to Tokyo to attend school of art. She brings the kitten along for its nice company. She keeps runt in her dormitory room in secret, as it is no pets allowed. Only shows it to a few people, so to make new friends by sharing with them a secret. It works. Friends come often, and sometimes bring treats runt enjoys to lick. Daifuku, red bean. Sometimes Makiko pours a little bit of tapioca juice into a small bowl for runt, too. Coconut. Runt dips its half-paw, then licks it like a popsicle. Makes a little mess, even makes a bowl stain on the dormitory desk. That's okay. Makiko is happy just like this.

One day, Makiko places a package of red bean on the shelf above her desk. While out at class, runt becomes curious. Sniffs his way up to the desk, where he sniffs the wall. For the first time, runt jumps, lands on the shelf, and finds daifuku. *Cool*, thinks runt. *To sniff, to jump high.* Runt touches the package with its half-paw. It falls from shelf to desk. At such a sound, runt's ears twitch. Feels powerful. But that is not all. Sniffs breeze from the window beside the shelf. Also, bits of other scents carried by it. What many more snacks can be sniffed? What many more plateaus exist from which to make things fall?

Runt must find out. Begins waiting at the door so to scoot out whenever Makiko comes and goes. Makiko becomes worried that one day she will not catch runt in time, and the dormitory supervisor will discover her secret. Becomes worried she will be kicked out of the dormitory, out of school of art. Tells all new friends please to knock before entering, so to give time for her to hide runt in the wardrobe. His ears twitch at every knock. He scoots as fast as he can but is always caught by Makiko. *The more I scoot, the more powerful I do become,* thinks runt. *I will escape. I will find the place beyond the dormitory room, the place from where the snack breeze does blow.*

Hiro, cousin of Makiko, works at Hōnto No Kimochi Gallery and Café in Setagaya City. One day, Hiro pays a visit to Makiko at the school of art. She takes the Odakyu Line from Umegaoka Station to Noborito Station, makes a change to Nambu Line, then makes a change again to Musashino Line. Brings along with her a flier for a contest she hopes Makiko will enter.

Hiro likes Makiko's paintings. Most of all, she likes the paintings of the beach in Fukuoka, where she grew up and did walks, too. Upon Hiro's arrival at the dormitory, she knocks on Makiko's door. No answer. She says, "Makiko?" Nothing. Inside, however, many twitches of runt's ears are happening. Hiro tries the door. It is unlocked. She opens the door, and out scoots runt, so fast he is not even noticed by Hiro. Amazed at his own power, runt is stunned. Feels freedom squeezing all his sides. Crouches low to the floor. In the dormitory, Hiro leaves the flyer on Makiko's desk, then passes by runt as she leaves. Runt catches a whiff of her shoes, same shoes Hiro wears when working at the café. Smells like daifuku, red bean.

Sniffing their path, runt follows close to Hiro, scooting at the pace of which she walks. Follows her all the way back to the station, where she finds there is now an issue with her previous train taken. Hiro doubles back to the street to board a bus. Runt follows still, scoots through doors and up onto the bus, hides beneath her seat, and enjoys a couple licks of her soles. Then, he follows Hiro off the bus, into the next station, through doors of a new train travelling a different route back to the cafe. But when the train does arrive at Kandu Station, runt finds himself amidst many sounds of feet, many different scents. Loses whiff of Hiro shoes. Hiro makes the change to the new train, and runt finds himself in a new place, outside, on a footpath.

Now, runt makes it his mission to find a safe place in which to make a cozy nest, and, he hopes, eat a snack. Scoots between feet of walking people, across a road, down an alleyway. In the alleyway, he sniffs out an empty box that once held pork bone. Thinks, *Good scent*. Thinks, *Would like to eat scent, sleep in scent*, and jumps inside. But here, he is met by another cat, who growls. Swats. Nicks runt, just a little. On the cheek. Runt jumps out. Keeps sniffing. Soon, sniffs his way through a tarp door flap, into the house of an artist stirring hot water over a bowl of ramen. Smells good. Real good. Pork bone. Also, fishy. To his own surprise, runt begins to vibrate. Never did before. He drops to the ground, rolls onto his back, and paws at the salty air.

The artist laughs. "Look at this cat!" he even says aloud to himself. "It is funny-looking! You want some ramen, cat? Here." He tosses a noodle to the floor. Runt flips over, sniffs. Finds the noodle and gobbles it up. *More*, he vibrates. "You want more?" says the artist. "Okay. Here." He tosses another noodle. Tosses a bit of tuna. Runt loves it. Runt cannot stop his body from vibrating. Licks his paw so to rub the fishy smell onto his face, and behind his ears.

"You are funny, cat," laughs the artist. Runt licks. "You and me, we make good friends."

And, for a little while, they do, runt and the artist. They make good friends. Behind the easel, while the artist paints, runt sleeps, or at least sits very still, while breathing very slow, because the artist cannot tell for sure if runt does ever sleep or not, with eyes always closed. Sometimes, the artist creates sculptures, and runt brushes against them. The artist laughs when bits of orange fur become stuck to the clay. Gives ramen whenever runt makes him laugh. After ramen, runt licks himself for a long time until covered in the scent of fish and fat, like wearing a fish and fat blanket. Some nights, they sleep on a tatami mat together. Other nights, the artist stays awake, howls around the alleyways with other howling friends. Those times, runt will perch upon an old sake barrel and wait. When the tarp flap opens, he hears the artist laughing, runt jumps down, brushes against his feet, vibrates, and the artist shares with him some more.

One day, the artist decides that he would like to paint for himself a portrait of runt. Arranges space so to stand the easel facing the sake barrel, whereupon he coerces runt to perch by placing a bit of tuna. Runt jumps to the barrel, eats the tuna, then happily lays his belly upon the fishy wood while the artist paints. On this one day, however, the artist receives a visitor. Friend passes by the window the artist cut into the tarp and covered with bamboo wood. Looks inside. Waves and holds up a cup to show the artist that they have brought a cup. The artist sets down his brush.

The artist rolls up the bamboo, says hello to his friend. Friend passes cup through. "I made it," they say. "Taste. Go on." The artist sips from the cup, then places it on the barrel beside runt. Runt sniffs a familiar scent. Coconut. Has Makiko found him? Has she come to take him back to the dormitory at the school of art? No. Runt does not want to go. He leaps from the barrel. Scoots through the tarp flap. Searches for a box to hide inside of. But each box he comes to growls back. Swats. Nicks. Runt sniffs the air, does not want to lose his way back to the artist. Yet, so many scents are dizzy-making. Chicken, octopus, squid, beer, chocolate. He crouches low to the ground. Thinks, *I am lost.* Thinks, *I am but small runt, wanting no more than for little snack. Please do not step on me.* Sniffs the air. Tries to sift through it for a fishy scent. Crawls in the direction of the first whiff he catches.

The artist, speaking through the window with his friend, does not at first notice the disappearance of runt. Friend tells many jokes to the artist, and the artist is distracted for some time, enjoying all his own laughter. When finally his friend carries onward, the artist still laughs, his eyes still drip tears, his belly still aches awhile. It takes some time for him to resettle behind the easel. Even then, it takes more time for his hands to steady enough so as to hold a brush, as the chuckles still peter out. As he dips the brush, he raises his gaze to the sake barrel. Sees runt is no longer perched in place. "Very funny," he says. "Very funny for you to hide on me." He gets up from his stool and goes to the bowl of ramen. Picks out a noodle and waves it around. "Sniff, sniff, funny-looking friend," he sing-songs. "Come and get your soup-soup."

No runt appears. The artist looks around his house. Not much place to look. Beneath a pile of garbage and things. Behind sculptures, other paintings. He goes out the tarp flap and circles the house, walks down the alleyway, and asks the people he meets, "Have you seen an orange cat? No eyes, half-paw foot. Real funny-looking." And the people say, "Yes, we did, we saw that ugly runt, he went that way," and point out the alleyway, toward another alleyway, where the artist continues to search, all the while holding his brush, dripping a trail of orange paint behind him.

*

One day, Makiko goes to see a new installation by the infamous artist BadDog as per a school of art assignment. BadDog, most well-known for his works in the genre of animalism, has most cleverly constructed a mural from human junk, as a way to be ironic, but also kind of true. Makiko takes a bus, then makes change to a train that arrives at Kandu Station, from where she will walk to Taitō Ward to find a mural displayed upon the shutters of an out-of-business tofu shop. At the first alleyway, however, Makiko sees a painting propped up on a sake barrel. The painting depicts a three-and-a-half-pawed, no-eyed cat with orange fur, perched in a sphinx position on the edge of a circular table, next to an orange cup with a square handle. Also, it reads: *My lost friend. Return to BadDog house if found. Much reward.*

Since his escape, Makiko had searched for runt every day in the gardens around the campus. She left little bits of red bean outside her dormitory door. She painted the beach where she had found him, over and over again, his skinny, deformed body curled in a cozy dune left by a footprint in the sand. "No," she says to passersby, who look at her funny as tears choke up her face. "No reward. That is my lost cat. Return him to me."

Makiko takes the painting with her that day, back to her dormitory at the school of art.

*

R.I.P. SCOOT

While visiting her friend Tenchi in the hospital in Fukuoka, Tacka receives a picture of a painting of a runt cat from her sister, Makiko, in Tokyo. *It's my cat. It looks just like him*, she attached to a phone message. Tacka shows the photo to Tenchi, as well as to Tenchi's cat Tacka had brought along to visit. In return, Tenchi sends to Makiko a video they had made with Tacka only moments prior to receiving the picture: *It looks just like her*, they write, in regards to Tenchi's cat, who, they do not even know, is the subject of the painting's mother. *But more blind and deformed.*

*

After following a whiff down one alley, then two, between booting feet of many people who yell, "Shoo," and, "Get away, rat," even though he is not a rat, but a cat, runt finds himself scooting up a ramp into the back of a delivery truck, where he hides behind large containers storing fish. Door of the truck is soon pulled down, and the engine starts. Runt cannot tell what is causing more vibrating, the truck, or his own body due to being amongst so much fish? The truck drives to shipping docks where soon the door rolls up again, and people who yell, "Why are you always late?" and "Move it," yell such things while taking away the containers of fish. Runt scoot outs from behind the feet of one such yelling person, and leaps from the bed of the truck. Outside of the truck now, the fishy scent is very strong. It's alive. Runt scoots along the dock, over yet another ramp, gangplank, onto the deck of a boat, where the scent is all over the floor. Scoots until he finds a cozy crack in which to hide amongst more containers. Rolls, vibrates, as a loud horn wails, and the ship pushes off to sea.

Out from between the containers creep more cats. And rats. Runt hears their yowls, squeaks. He stays in his spot. Wonders why the ground moves so much in this fishy, salty place. It never feels still. Even his own fur and skin feels like it moves, like it crawls all over itself. Runt itches. Runt chews at bits of fur. Perhaps he sleeps? He doesn't know. For can he be sleeping if he is still scratching?

Finally, after many days, the horn wails again. The ground heaves, then the movement stops. Loud sounds of birds. Again, runt hears many feet of people around him. He scoots in wobbles along the edge of the deck, following the footstep sounds. Perhaps they will lead to a place with a fishy scent, but without persistent motion and itching? He follows feet over a gangplank, off the boat, until he is scooped up by a person who carries him like a dangling snake, his back feet dragging against the ground. This person laughs a lot, like the artist, but squeakier sounding like a rat. An artist rat? Soon, they drop runt, and he scoots over yet another ramp, hoping to find a place to hide, itch and chew. Another horn wails. The movement of the ground begins again.

*

Runt spends three weeks sleeping in the tween deck, eating skins and fat scraps from the scullery at night. When voices are more quiet, footsteps are not around, he scoots around the main deck, even chasing the scuttle sounds of cockroaches. The occasional mouse. He grows used to his life at sea. To constant movement. Even on his skin. Then one day, finally, the horn wails for the last time. Movement stops. Loud birds. Runt realizes, once again, he has a chance to scoot free. Listens for people's feet and follows them down gangplank. On land now, runt sniffs the new air. Cold and fresh. He keeps sniffing to find new a snack.

First whiff he catches: coconut. Is he close to the dormitory again? Or the sake barrel? Doesn't know. Follows the scent until he finds himself confronted by a yipping dog. Runt swats his half-paw. Feels the hot breath from the dog on patches of his skin. Backs up. More yipping, and a person yelling. "Oh my god," they yell. A bell falls to the ground. Jingles, runt hears. Next, feels tapioca juice fall onto his skin. Runt scoots away. Licks the juice. Then hears new feet come close. They stop. The little bell is picked up. Runt follows after its jingle.

Soon, though, there are many horns. Many engines and things. Many sirens. Runt scoots between feet, trying to follow the jingle, but the jingle becomes lost. Runt cannot hear. He searches for a new whiff which to catch and follow. Soon he does catch something new. Something sweet. Like daifuku, almost. Almost like red bean. Also, he hears sounds like the bell, but more calm. More rattle-like. They are going fast, though. *Wait*, thinks runt. *You are where I want to go*, and scoots extra so to catch up. But before he can, he is scooped once again like a dangling snake. This time, though, he dangles much higher from the ground.

"My new baby," says the scooper. He is placed inside a cold, wiry rocking space. It is very loud, the metal, and high-pitched screaming from its wheels hurts his ears. Loses the gentle sound, the sweet whiff. Runt sinks low against the bottom of this new cage. Feels like a box, but worse, with holes in the bottom his paws get jammed in. Then feels the fur of another cat. The other cat snarls, extra nasty. Gives runt a nick. A small bite, too. Runt shifts back against the side of the cage, hard and painful against his skin. Is still. Waits many blocks until rocking and screaming comes to a stop.

Weird whiff now. Like many different scents dumped together. But not appetizing. Not vibration-making. Rotten. *Can I jump high out of here?* thinks runt. He tries. Leaps out and is followed by the yell of the scooper. "Help, my baby!" But no one helps. Runt scoots behind the scent blender, hides. An animal with a twitchy tail leaps from the dumpster and lands on runt's head, however. To his own surprise, runt makes a hissing noise for the first time, like a real snake. Uses his full paw to pin down the tail of the animal, which in turn does make many screeches of fear. Runt never has felt before this feeling. To be a hunter. Even more power. Then the scooper rushes over, grabs the animal by its body, and tugs. "That's mine!" they yell at runt. "My new baby. Give it to me!" The screeching is unbearable. Runt digs in his nails. Scooper tugs hard. Animal splits. Runt chews the tail from his paw, scoots away with it dangling from his mouth.

Over a curb, between vehicles parked in rows, then down a laneway from where the echoes of grunts and bolts lifting echo. John, resident at 888 Dupont, pushes a cinder block in front of a steel door so to keep the door propped open while he goes to replace his broken key. As runt scoots closer, he catches a whiff. Salty, fishy. It's ramen. He scoots inside. Follows the whiff through a crawlspace, up many narrow steps into a room with a trap door ajar. Butts through. Paws open the door of the room, and scoots into a hallway, where the whiff leads him to yet another door. Paws at that door. Hears footsteps. Door opens. He drops the tail from his mouth.

*

One day Tenchi, owner of the cat that is the mother of runt, finally dies. To Tacka, Yasushi the gardener gifts an orchid in their memory. Said Tenchi always reminded him of an orchid, due to their different hairstyles, always so chic. Tacka agrees. So much so, it sends shivers through her, the orchid. Knowing it would soon go to sleep for a long time, she takes her flower home and photographs it, wanting to keep a vision of its likeness with her for the winter.

Makiko, thinking Tenchi was right about the cat in the painting, that it did look just like theirs, minus two eyes and half a paw, keeps the BadDog painting for herself on the shelf above the dormitory desk. For now, her lost runt feels like the lost Tenchi. Both feel present within the art. A cat, and a shadow passing by a window.

*

At home, Sarah arrives with another package, sets it on top of others at the bottom of the shelf.

Then she fertilizes my orchid, already sleeping.

*

After scooting between his feet and curling itself into a circle upon a wool sweater lumped on his floor, Austin, the other resident at 888 Dupont, gives runt a name: *Scoot*. Scoot is happy with this. Scoot licks his itchy tail. He vibrates, and then he falls asleep.

I can tell you, he wanted to stay.

Door is left open for the first time in the whole life of Frida. Why? To tease Frida? Or, to finally set her free? What is that crazy lady thinking? Don't know, but there she goes, anyway, Frida, through it, through the broken boards of the back fence. She squeezes. On the other side of the fence, she finds open space. Pavement. A loading docks for trucks. No one around, so Frida hops onto the bed of one. Where is the guy? Taking a break? She sees the purple star on a box of Party Mix cat treats. Then many purple stars, many boxes of Party Mix cat treats, as she looks upward, and around. She scratches the box. Scratches it lots. Wants those treats real bad. Then the truck door rolls shut. Engine starts. Guy's back to work now. Headed up to the border.

Acknowledgements

Many thanks to the Canada Council for the Arts and the Ontario Arts Council for supporting this work; to Sam Hiyate at The Rights Factory and the team at Nightwood Editions for their dedication to bringing this project to life; to Anna Comfort O'Keeffe for the bomb cover design; and to Janine Young for her tireless editorial efforts and immaculate sense of humour—how lucky I have been to have ended up here.

To my family and friends who continue to champion my work no matter how weird it gets; to Mark, whose love for a cat inspired this story; to Yasushi, whose painting of a cat also inspired this story; and to Chopper and Little Bear for showing up right when I needed you the most—thank you all from the deepest parts of my heart.

Finally, much love to the city of Toronto, its curious laneways, and all of the exceptional characters that make this place so good. Nowhere else in the world feels more like home.